The characters and events portrayed in this book are fictitious. Any resemblance to actual persons, living or dead, business establishments, events or locales is entirely coincidental.

The Earl's Hired Bride
Copyright 2016 by Deb Marlowe
Cover Design by Lily Smith

For my Great-Uncle Ed, who was funny and kind and who told me many times that I was the spitting image of my Grandma when she was a girl.

Prologue
Half Moon House
April, 1817

"The gentleman did not give his name."

Hestia Wright shared a glance with her boulder of a footman. She and Isaac had been together for years. They both knew that the number of gentlemen who wished not to advertise his association with her was legion.

The man in her office could be anyone. Perhaps not a former protector—the majority of them were too wealthy and influential to appear unnoticed here in Craven Street. A present business associate or charitable sponsor, then? Or a future benefactor for the work they did at Half Moon House? The twinkle in Isaac's eye told her that there was something special about this one.

Even so, she was caught by surprise when she breezed into her office.

"Your Grace," she said with pleasure. She dipped into the elegant curtsy that had once been envied and imitated in Europe's finest parlors. "What an unexpected but delightful surprise."

The Duke of Danby rose from the chair before her desk. He bowed, but it was an impatient gesture. "I'm sorry to burst in on you unannounced and without an appointment, but no one knows I'm in Town yet."

"Well, I did not know," she said with a smile, "which means that indeed, likely no one does."

"I'd like to keep it that way, for just a little while longer," he said with a significant glance at Isaac.

"Your Grace," Hestia chided. "You know we are the souls of discretion. Your secrets are safe with us."

"I do know it—and that is why I am here."

"Come and sit." She waved him away from the desk and toward the grouping of chairs before the fire. "Let us be comfortable. Isaac will bring tea."

"You are still a stunningly beautiful woman, Hestia," he said bluntly as they settled into their seats.

"Thank you." She flashed him a smile. "I'm not the young sylph I was when we assisted each other with that matter in Prague, so long ago."

"But you are ten times the woman, by all reports." The Duke leaned in. "Which is why I am here to ask for your help once again. And yes, before you ask, I'm ready to give you a sizable donation for your good works, in exchange."

"Oh, dear. Not even a negotiation? I do remember our collaboration, Your Grace. You make me worry that this must be a difficult task indeed."

"It is," he admitted. "It's a damned tricky business."

Isaac knocked and Hestia called for him to enter. She watched the duke fidget while she poured. When they were both served she sat back and eyed him over the rim of her cup.

"I've done my best by my family," he said as the door closed behind her footman. "It's important to me. It hasn't been easy, but I've managed to negotiate most of the younger generation into alliances with solid spouses of good character and situation."

"And bullied and manipulated when negotiation failed, if the gossips have it right?"

"Gossips be damned. My family is by and large ready to continue on in happiness and prosperity. It's a worthwhile life's work, if you ask me. But there are a few cases left—and I'm here about a particularly delicate one."

"Do tell," she invited.

He set down his cup. "This is for your ears only, you understand."

"You have my word," she assured him.

"You will perhaps have heard of my sister Georgina?"

Hestia knew the family history of most of the important houses in England and Europe— and a great many of their secrets, too. She suspected she was about to discover a new one.

"I have heard of her. Her name has been mentioned of late, mostly due to your success in marrying her granddaughter off to the new Lord Ellesworth. Congratulations, by the way."

He nodded his thanks. "What have you heard of Georgina, then?"

Hestia frowned thoughtfully. "Let me recall . . . She was married to Charles Bolton, the great adventurer and scholar, correct?"

"Yes. It was a sensation, back in its day. Charles was a dashing, intelligent, handsome man. No one questioned why she wanted him." He took a sip of tea. "What they should have wondered, and did not, was why she was allowed to choose him."

"I should think the Whitton stubbornness was explanation enough."

"It appears it was. But it wasn't the real explanation."

Hestia stilled.

"Yes, you've guessed it aright, I see. Georgina was compromised." He held up a hand. "She was not harmed. She didn't suffer physically, at least." He sighed. "She fancied herself in love with a scoundrel though, as some girls are wont to do. He seduced her, got her in the family way and then demanded a snoot full of money to keep it quiet."

"He wouldn't marry her?" Hestia let her surprise show.

"He might have, but she wouldn't have him once she discovered his true colors. She vowed she'd whelp in a barn and live there rather than face a lifetime tied to a liar and a vile betrayer."

"As I said, the Whitton stubbornness."

He nodded. "We most all of us live with a dose of it—and Georgina had more than most. A family consult was held, and my grandmother—a wicked wit of a harridan herself—took her off *on tour* to hide the situation. They let it out that they were for Europe, but headed north instead. A couple in Edinburgh was found to take the child. He was a successful linen draper, and well able to take good care of the girl."

"Ah. Charles Bolton was from Edinburgh as well, was he not?"

Danby sighed. "Yes. He was home from one adventure or another and met Georgina while she lingered there, recovering. They were smitten from the first, or so the story goes. My sister learned from her mistakes, though, I'll give her that. She took it slow with him—and she told him the truth about the babe. It didn't deter him. In fact, they pledged to continue anonymous support for her—and they did, until she was grown and married."

"Your sister was lucky—as was her daughter. I know so very many other women for whom things did not turn out so well."

"Yes, well, that's just it. I don't think it's ended." Danby's expression grew pained, but his tone remained earnest. "I never knew the full extent of the story until I stepped into the dukedom and by then it was over. I admit—I've had occasional pangs over it. After all, there's a woman out there somewhere, my niece by blood, if not law." He trailed off. "I made a few enquiries, once, when I had business in Edinburgh. The girl had moved on, though, and no one was left who could say where. I figured it was for the best."

"And what has changed now?"

"I got a note from an old friend, who reported seeing a girl here in London. Young. And reputed to be the very image of Georgina."

"I see." Hestia thought that could very well mean something . . . or it could not.

"I thought at first that he must have encountered Glenna in her bookshop or about Town. She does bear a resemblance, although her hair has that auburn tint that Georgina's never had."

"But you don't believe so now?"

"I got a second note last week—from a different acquaintance. Glenna hasn't been in London since Christmas, as you know. She removed to Ellesworth's estate right after the marriage. My friend remarked on the uncanny likeness the girl bore my sister—even down to the same thick, ebony hair."

Hestia sat, silent.

"I came to investigate."

"And you found . . . ?"

"There can be no doubt. I lay in wait at the park where my friend had seen her. We waited together and it took two days—just two old men loitering in the sun. We spotted her—and I swear I was transported back in time. I wouldn't have been surprised if she marched up and scolded me for spoiling her doll's dress. She *must* be Georgina's granddaughter."

"You wouldn't be here if it were that simple, Your Grace. What happened?"

His hand shook, just the slightest bit, as he sipped his tea. "She was dressed . . . like a servant. Or perhaps not that well. Just slightly better than a street urchin. She looked thin. You know the hungry look I mean, more than most." He shook his head. "It rattled me."

"Did you approach her?"

"I tried. The chit saw me. I got the notion that she knew who I was—and wanted none of me. She turned immediately and blended into the crowd. I followed. I'm not so old as to be given the slip by a bit of a girl."

"Of course not."

"I found her, but she's a wily one. She stood at the gate to the street and stared back at me. She shook her head at me, the minx. And then she jumped on the back of a hackney like she'd done it countless times before—and disappeared." He slumped back in his seat. "But it doesn't add up. She was in the park by herself—in the fashionable hour. If she's a maid, wouldn't she have been with her employer?" He closed his eyes. "A grand-niece of mine—a maid. Or worse."

He sat up suddenly and met Hestia's gaze. "I will have her found."

"To what end, Your Grace?" What do you intend to do with her?" Hestia was reliably sure she knew the answer to that already.

"I will see her settled, of course." He shuddered. "Wipe that look off of her face."

"Married?" she asked gently.

He raised his brow and gave her a very *ducal* look. "Were you not listening, my dear? It is what I do. She'll be brought into the fold.

And she'll be married—into happiness and prosperity."

Hestia favored him with a healthy dose of skepticism. "That is a tall order, sir. I see why you sought my help."

He nodded. "You've got contacts in every layer of London. If anyone can help me bring this about, it is you, Hestia."

"True. Together, we might achieve it. In a far different manner than what you are accustomed to, though, sir. You are going to have to give me some leeway." She steepled her fingers together. "This is going to take a very particular sort of gentleman." She shot him a look. "Do you have someone in mind?"

"No, more's the pity. Do you?"

"Not yet. But give me a few days." She smiled slowly. "I do love a challenge."

Chapter One

Light spilled into the street. The theatre was lit up like a beacon. Swinging carriage lamps and torches carried by footmen further brightened the area—as did the sparkle of embroidery and jewels on the ladies and gentlemen moving to ascend the broad steps.

Emily Spencer stepped out of the shadows. "Excuse me, miss. You dropped this from your reticule."

The grandly dressed young woman raked her with a bored gaze, took in the rough, ill-fitting linen of her dress and the dirty cloth hiding her hair. She looked away. "It's not mine. You are mistaken."

Emily did not let rudeness deter her. She stared with admiration at the young woman's gown, allowed her eyes to wander upward, and gave a happy little gasp. "Oh, my! Are you not Miss Paxton? You are even more beautiful than I have heard!"

The young lady's head swiveled back, her expression warmer. "Thank you. Yes, I am indeed Miss Paxton."

"Oh, how wonderful! And your dress! It's so beautiful. Surely it will be described in the papers." She focused on the sheer overskirt. "How cunning that garland is, how beautifully embroidered!" Emily deliberately looked up, then. "And it is repeated on your headdress. I'm sure you'll start a new fashion, Miss Paxton!"

In fact, Emily was more than passing familiar with that particular embroidery. She'd been present for many hours while her own mother labored over it. She'd also been on the premises of one of London's preeminent modistes, making a delivery, when Miss Paxton had returned the bill for the garment, including a note stating that the dress was unsatisfactory, and not fit to be worn.

"You'll be dictating fashion when you are a countess, Miss, won't you? Many congratulations to you on your engagement!" Emily bobbed a curtsy. "The streets are full of talk of your splendid match."

The ice descended once more. "Thank you." The young lady turned her back and stepped forward.

"Oh, but wait . . ." Emily allowed a mask of confused dismay to wash over her. "Your betrothed is the Earl of Ardman, so why would you be carrying a gentleman's handkerchief with *these* initials?" She ran a finger over the MLH stitched onto the linen.

Emily knew very well why—because Miss Paxton was engaging in some very illicit behavior with Marcus Lionel Holt—the middle-aged earl's younger cousin.

"Hush, you meddlesome creature." Miss Paxton had turned back. "That doesn't belong to me, I told you." Her eyes narrowed. "But give it to me and get from my sight."

"Oh, Miss Paxton!" Emily's voice ranged a bit higher. "Tell me you never stepped out on your betrothed?" She pressed the hanky to her mouth, hoping the linen hid her nerves and allowing the initials to face outward. At least she didn't worry that it might be unclean. After all, she had purchased and embroidered it herself.

Miss Paxton snatched at the offending piece of linen.

Emily stepped back, out of reach. "You did!" she wailed accusingly. "You played the Earl of Ardman for a fool!"

"Lower your tone, you tiresome troublemaker!" The lady was glancing about now—and beginning to truly worry.

There. That was the look Emily had been waiting for.

"I will." She dropped the subservient, eager-to-please note completely. "For five pounds."

Miss Paxton gasped. "Why you grasping little cheat!"

"Katharine, come along!" The stout matron ahead beckoned Miss Paxton. "We do not dawdle in the street!"

"Ten pounds," Emily said flatly. "Or I start to cry about the poor, mistreated earl. Loudly. In detail." She steeled her nerves and tilted her head. "I could mention that tryst in Green Park, perhaps? The one in which Mr. Holt tore the sleeve of the rose under-dress you wore beneath a green pelisse?"

"I don't have ten pounds." Miss Paxton could barely speak for gritting her teeth.

"Ladies do not carry such vulgar amounts of money."

Emily raised her chin. "Nor do they carry on in such vulgar ways in the shrubbery." She pursed her lips. "An earring will do—if those diamond chips are real."

"Of course they are real. As is the ruby!" Miss Paxton's face had gone red with outrage. "Even one is worth far more than ten pounds!"

"Is it worth more than your betrothal?" Emily asked heartlessly. She *hoped* she sounded heartless—and convincing. "I won't get its full worth when I pawn it, in any case."

Miss Paxton speared her with a deadly glare. Emily gave her credit. She showed more spunk than she had expected—growing angry instead of dissolving into a teary puddle of guilt and fear. Good heavens, she would never have had the spine to stand there emanating hatred and calculation.

Luckily, the reckoning went Emily's way. Without another word the heiress removed the earring and tossed it at her.

Emily caught it with shaking fingers and tucked it away.

"Give me the kerchief," her victim hissed.

"No." Emily turned to go. "I'll think I will keep it for insurance."

She walked off into the dark, leaving Miss Paxton fuming behind her—and telling herself that she felt not a smidgen of remorse. Girls like Miss Paxton did not deserve it. She'd been born with everything—health, wealth, a large, warm home, fine clothes, a name that meant something, and a family that cared for and wanted the best for their daughter. So she'd been engaged to an older man? By all accounts the Earl of Ardman was a kind man, a good caretaker of his properties, a fair lord to his servants and tenants. Perhaps the gentleman had lost a few hairs—he also had a ready smile and a good heart and a willingness to lay them all at Miss Paxton's feet. And she had repaid him with betrayal.

Nothing riled Emily Spencer more than watching a person in possession of a treasure willfully toss it aside.

She stuffed the linen into a pocket as she left the scene. It was still in good shape. She could pick out the initials and use it again—if she could stiffen her backbone enough to try something like this again.

"She's a stone-cold 'un, ain't she?" The boy, several years younger than she, melted out of the darkness to walk at Emily's side.

"Yes. Be sure to steer clear of her. I don't want her to catch a glimpse of you and figure out that you had a hand in watching her."

Jasper shrugged. "I talked to Finch. He'll open early and said for ye to come to the back door."

"Thank you."

"They looked real sparkly in the street lights," he said eagerly. "Will we get the month's rent out of it, d'ye think?"

"First thing, we must give the modiste her share for that gown. It's only fair, even if she doesn't know how or where the money came from. But we should cover this month, and next month too, as long as long as Miss Paxton has not played her family as false as she played her betrothed.”

“No fancy mort could be that wicked,” Jasper said cheerfully. “We’ll be on easy street for the next few weeks, Em!”

“I hope so, Jasper.” She thought of her mother’s fingers, lying still in her lap while she rested her head against a window frame. “I hope so.”

* * *

“Paste!” Mr. Finch announced with a shake of his head. “What is the world coming to when the young ladies wear paste to the theatre?”

Emily’s heart sank. “I should have known,” she groaned. “It’s what I get for allowing myself to sink to her level.”

The fence gave an apologetic shrug. “I can take it apart, make something *new* and fake out of it—but I can only give you a few shillings.”

“I’ll take what I can get, I suppose.” Emily fought back a surge of despair. She wouldn’t have pulled such a trick had she not been desperate. But her mother was growing thinner and more tired by the day. She’d given up full-scale sewing several months ago, leaving Emily to fill those few orders they could get from busy modistes. Emily had convinced her mother to restrict herself to the fancy ribbon embroidery she was so skilled at—and that was still popular with both the modistes and the high-end milliners.

But her mother's fingers moved slower these days. She didn't walk out to take the air like she used to, but stayed at the window, working longer hours—and producing fewer finished pieces. Emily knew she wasn't eating well. Their meals were meager enough, and still her mother slipped some of her share to Jasper, or tried to push it on her daughter.

They couldn't go on like this. Emily wouldn't allow it. Her mother was the sweetest, gentlest soul that ever lived and Emily would not allow her to fade away—even if she had to get up to a bit of wickedness to prevent it.

An image flashed in her head—of her near encounter in the park the other day. She sighed. No, not even if she had to swallow her pride.

But, oh, what a bitter pill it would be, going down.

She took the meager payment from Mr. Finch and set out. She had deliveries to make today. As did Jasper, who made money acting as an errand and delivery boy for several milliners and modistes, and even a tailor in Saville Row. She met him at the corner, near Bond Street. Her heart sank again as she met his hopeful gaze with a shake of her head.

"Who would have thought it?" he asked mournfully after she'd delivered the bad news. "Miss Paxton wearing fake jewels—and her from one of the highest families in the land?" He sniffed. "Though Mr. Waters has griped that her papa is none too quick at paying his shot, either."

"I should have come up with a different scheme," Emily sighed, taking a few of his burdens from him.

"I'll keep my ear out for more gossip," Jasper offered. "We might yet try again."

"Perhaps."

They walked in silence for a moment. "Are you for Madame Lalbert's?" she asked.

"Yes. I'm to deliver a ball gown to Mayfair."

"She sent word to Mama yesterday that she has some ribbons she wishes enhanced. I'm to pick them up. I hope I can talk her into at least an over-slip as well."

"Well, keep your blinkers peeled," Jasper warned. "I notice the new head wrap. It looks dowdy enough. Had any further sign of the old gentleman?"

"No, not since I spotted him roving up and down Bond Street." She shook her head. 'He must have tracked down that jarvey that caught me hitching a ride. Can you imagine the money and manpower he must have expended, to find that driver?"

It sent shivers down her spine. The Duke of Danby. Why should he spend so much time and effort trying to find her? "What on earth do you think he wants?"

Jasper glowered. "Nothing good. Not his sort."

"You should have seen him, Jasper. He must be twice Mama's age, and yet you would think them contemporaries."

"It's what a lifetime of country air, good food and plenty o' blunt will do for ye," the boy said sagely.

"Yes, and an absence of cares and worries. And if he can offer Mama any of that, then perhaps we should let him?"

Jasper scoffed. "That old toff ain't here to do ye any favors, Em, and ye know it. More like he means to run ye right out o' Town." They ducked down the alley that would take them to the back entrance to the modiste's shop. "It's exactly why Molly Standon left. The family came fer the Season and wanted no chance that the younger generation would catch a glimpse of her, waltzing about London looking fer all the world the very image of their father."

"You might be right. But I don't look overly like him, nor does mama. So he might have a kinder purpose in mind."

"If he did, why wait until now?" Jasper shook his head and held open the door for her. "I'm telling ye, that toff's up to no good, should ye ask me."

"Which toff is that?" Madame Lalbert asked. She stood at a table in her backroom, tying a decorative bow around a large dress box.

Jasper eyed the girl cutting into a jonquil silk at the next table and shrugged.

Madame Lalbert shifted her gaze from him, to Emily and back. "Josephine," she said thoughtfully, "will you run up to the storage room and bring down that white Brussels lace we bought last week? I'm thinking it will look well with that promenade dress."

The seamstress rose and left the room and Madame crossed her arms over her formidable bosom. "Let's hear it."

Jasper explained while Emily fidgeted. "Do you think there's a chance that he means well?" she asked when her friend had finished.

The modiste sighed. "That one? I don't know. The old duke is notorious for being picky about his family. He runs riot over the lot of them, it's said, bullying and manipulating until he's got them married off to his satisfaction."

"Well, he can't want to marry Mama off, nor me. Why would he interfere in our lives, after all of this time?"

Before he died, her papa had asked her to be gentle, if the topic of her mama's real parents ever came up. "She never got over thinking they might come and enquire after her," he'd said. It had explained finally, just what her mother was longing for, when she grew quiet and that dreamy, hungry look came over her. It had explained the hopeful tone with which she'd always greeted new customers in their storefront, and the tiny wrinkle of disappointment that always creased her brow, as if she was continually waiting for someone who never came.

Madame shook her head. "I'm sure I could not guess, but the man has such a reputation for being crotchety and insistent on his own way, I would be careful, were I you."

Emily nodded, her protective instincts surging. That was not the sort of man whom her mother dreamed of, she felt sure. "I will be careful. Mama is fragile enough, without having her heart broken, too." She sighed. "But I cannot very well stay inside all day. We need the work."

"Speaking of which, here is the ribbon I wish to have embroidered." She fetched a roll of blue silk. "It's for a sash. I'd like that garland motif that your mother does so well, in darker blues and greys. And for you," she turned to Jasper, "that box needs to go to Lord Dayle's in Bruton Street."

Emily bargained a moment, managing to convince the modiste that she'd need a trim to go with a matching spencer or pelisse, as well, and then she and Jasper set out again. They would have to split ways soon enough, and were making plans to meet up again in the afternoon, when a pair of boys tumbled out of a shop right in front of them.

"Three Fingered Jack!" one cried, holding his flat, wrapped package high.

The other thrust a victorious fist in the air, "The Terror of Jamaica!"

Emily laughed, then quickly stepped around them when a little girl and a young woman emerged to join them.

Jasper elbowed her as they moved on. "Ain't that the one in the park? The one we seen Miss Paxton snub?"

"Yes, poor thing. She looked devastated, too." She'd seen the incident and felt sorry for the girl. "Miss Paxton only cut her because of her unfortunate gown," she whispered.

Jasper was looking back over his shoulder. "It didn't learn her nuthin'. She's dressed no better today."

Emily had seen. "Miss Carmichael, I think, is her name." Again, she looked a fright in a walking dress too large, too out of date and covered with too many questionable frills and furbelows.

It was too bad. She seemed amiable and kind. Looking back, Emily watched her usher her brothers and sister along with patience and smiles. Lord Ardman would have done better to choose a girl like this over a cat like Miss Paxton. But the vainglorious gentlemen of the *ton* would always flock to a fashion plate over a quiz, would they not?

Poor girl. She was likely the victim of an unskilled, untutored village seamstress with a collection of old fashion magazines. She only needed someone knowing to take her in hand and she'd strike a far better note with the young bucks.

She stopped suddenly. Now, was that not a thought?

"Are ye comin'?" Jasper asked.

"No. I think I'm going back to discuss something with Madame Lalbert."

"Suit yerself." Jasper lifted his chin. "See you tonight!"

Emily nodded and started back the way they'd come. Perhaps, just perhaps, she'd hit upon a scheme that would let her turn things around without selling her soul or sacrificing her pride.

Chapter Two

Cole Herrington, the Earl of Hartford, accepted the coat his footman held out. "Tell them not to wait dinner on me, Williams. The lecture is all the way out at Hampstead. I'll be late getting back."

"A moment, before you leave, my lord?"

Hart's head was full of weights, bushels, and triple yield barley. Most of his fellow peers would be bored witless at the thought of attending a session on the development of disease-resistant, higher-yield grain, but Hart was eager to implement new strains and practices. Impatient, he paused. "Yes? What is it?"

"Ah, well . . ." Williams cleared his throat. "A young person has been dawdling outside, just up the street. I thought you might wish to ah, take precautions."

"I understand." Damn it all! He'd scarcely been in Town but a few days. Was last Season's circus to start up again, and so soon? "Very well, Williams," he said curtly. "Alert my mother, if you please. And you come out with me to the street. It will be just as we practiced."

"Yes, sir." Williams gestured for a maid to run for the countess, then he put his hand on the door latch and took a deep breath. "Ready, sir?"

"No. But open it anyway."

Hart went out, feeling the footman's presence right on his heel. He spotted the young lady. She'd stepped out smartly when the door opened. She began to fumble with her reticule, but Hart saw her glance up once, and again, gauging her steps.

As she'd obviously planned, they reached the pavement in front of Herrington House at the same time. As he'd suspected, her arms flew up, right on cue. She stumbled toward him—

And he stepped back and aside even as Williams slid into his place and caught the girl as she fell.

"Oh!" she cried as the servant lowered her to the ground. "My ankle!" She cast a distressed gaze up—and looked blatantly surprised to find herself in the arms of the footman. "Oh."

The front door flew open. Hart looked over and beckoned his mother. "Do you see?" he demanded, pointing at the girl.

"Oh, I can feel my ankle swelling," she moaned. "If someone could just help me up . . .?"

No one answered her.

"Oh, dear." Hart's mother bit her lip. "I did hope you were wrong, darling."

"As did I," he said grimly. "But clearly I am not to be given a moment's peace."

"Excuse me?" The girl was getting frustrated now. Clearly she'd expected a more receptive audience. "My ankle?"

"Yes, yes. We'll get you taken care of in a moment." His mother turned back to him. "You tried to fix the situation, but I don't know what we can do, now that . . . it hasn't worked out."

"I know what we can do," he said shortly. "Take her inside, Williams."

"Oh, thank you, my lord." The girl lifted a hand to him. "If you could just help me rise?"

He ignored her. "I'm going to put a stop to this before it gets out of hand."

"I'll see to her, but what about you, darling?" His mother sounded a little alarmed.

"Keep her. As long as you like. Nurse her, call her family, but warn them to leave the special license at home. I won't be back. Not until I have this matter in hand."

* * *

Not quite an hour later Hart strode up to the house on Craven Street. The famous half moon and stars, carved out of the fanlight and replaced with crystal, sparkled as the door swung open.

The woman emerging must be Hestia Wright. Surely there were not two such stunning women running about London. He stepped up. "Miss Wright? Forgive my bad manners, but may I detain you for a moment?"

The beautiful blonde smiled up at him. "Only for a moment. And please, call me Hestia. Mr.—?"

He bowed. "Lord Hartford, at your service, ma'am."

"My lord, I am ever so pleased to meet you, but I am in a bit of a hurry. If you would care to come back, or to step inside to make an appointment?"

"I do apologize. I am in a rush, myself." Desperate, he raked his hand through his hair and looked down toward the Strand. "Look, allow me to get you a hackney, then perhaps we can talk on the way?"

"No need." She gestured toward the coach ambling toward them. "Here is my carriage, but if you are in dire straits, then, of course, you may ride with me—as long as you promise not to interfere when I reach my destination."

Startled, he promised, then saw her into the coach and climbed in after her. "Many thanks to you, ma'am—"

"Just Hestia, please." She smiled at him and he lost a moment to the dazzle of it.

"Yes, of course. I'm afraid I must seem absurd to you, but I fear I'm in the midst of a situation that has descended to the level of a farce. I am indeed growing desperate."

"Normally I'd scoff, hearing such drama from a man like you, but I do remember a bit of what happened to you last Season." She regarded him steadily. "I take it you fear a repeat?"

"Yes, exactly!" He was relieved to find her so easy to talk with—and to find an air of understanding and steely competence under all of that ethereal beauty. He hoped like hell that she would put it to use for him.

"Tell me," she said simply.

"Well, what went on last Season was a disgrace," Hart said bitterly. "I never expected to inherit. My brother was the perfect heir. I was the perfect spare—little to be seen."

She chuckled.

"It was such a blow, losing him so young and so unexpectedly," he continued. "We were all still in shock. My brother's body was barely cold. I'd just been ceremoniously introduced into the House of Lords. I wasn't going about in Society, which apparently frustrated the young ladies of the ton."

"They can be an excitable lot," Hestia murmured.

"So I've learned. I was still trying to catch my breath, recover from having all of my plans yanked out from under me, and I'd barely begun learning all that my brother had been in training for all of his life. The last thing I wished to consider was marriage."

"Ah, but marriage is the only thing so many of these young ladies have to consider."

"Yes," he agreed darkly, "and apparently it caused a few of them to lose their minds."

She laughed.

"It was no laughing matter, I assure you. It started innocently enough. I wasn't attending parties or balls, so the young ladies tried to meet me in the street. They hung about my tailor's shop. They gathered in the gallery to watch sessions in the House and lingered in the halls. They dropped handkerchiefs and poems and invitations."

"And one, I recall, threw herself in front of your horse."

"That was only the beginning. Another threw herself from *her* horse into my arms. And one dropped from a tree right in front of me."

"Good heavens. How inventive."

"I gave up and left Town for Hartsworth Park—before somebody got killed."

"Yes, well." Hestia looked at him with a frank expression. "You are certainly an attractive young man, my lord. And your family is respectable, your title old, and your bank accounts are reportedly healthy. And yet, with all of that to recommend you, I think you must realize that none of it was what excited such a level of frenzy."

"I do know that, Hestia. None of these lunatic girls are truly interested in me. They all want to be mistress of Hartsworth."

"Everyone wants to be mistress of Hartsworth, sir. It is an irresistible notion. The most celebrated home in England, in a beautiful setting—"

"And immortalized by that damned poem."

"That wonderfully romantic, tragic poem, full of thwarted lovers and sacrifice and happily ever afters. Every girl in England sighs over that tale, dreams of a love so daring and bold, yearns to live out her own happiness, as is promised to all those who hold Hartsworth. They cut their teeth on the idea before they are out of the school room—and never lose the taste of the dream."

"Nicholas thwarted them all by engaging himself to a local girl at quite a young age."

"He cheated them of their chance. And then you appeared, unattached and uninterested. Clearly they were driven to extremes."

"Yes, well. I'm afraid extreme is not a trait I would ever look for in a bride."

She tilted her head. "Some would, you know. But you do seem remarkably even tempered, my lord."

"My mother says I'm as even keeled as a becalmed ship. I suppose all of those chits would find me boring, did they bother to get to know me. I'm far more interested in making Hartsworth pay for itself than in the romance associated with it."

"Yes, many would find that a disappointment," she agreed.

"Nor would they be interested in the amount of work needed to keep the old place going. Someone should tell them to forget the long list of lovers and think of the ancient plumbing that needs replaced and the glass that must be custom crafted to fit all of those arrow slits."

"What are plumbing and drafts next to thrills of the heart, my lord?" she asked with a smile. "So, you fear that the drama from last year will be repeated. It's a wonder that you came to Town at all."

"If I could have skipped it, I would have, believe me," he said fervently. "But although I never wished for the earldom, it's been thrust upon me—and I'll damned well do my best with it. I'm here to take my seat in the Lords. Not only because it is a duty, but also because I hope to address some issues that will affect

Hartsworth and several of the other estates I must look after."

"I'm sure you'll make a splendid earl. But now, why don't you tell me what has brought you to me in a state of desperation?"

"It's begun already. I've been in Town but a few days, and already two carriages have mysteriously broken down in our street. And today!" He told her the tale and fervently appreciated the fact that she didn't laugh.

"Oh, you are in a quandary," she sighed.

"Yes, and it's doubly bitter because I thought I'd found a solution."

Her eyebrows raised. "How is that?"

He couldn't suppress a sigh. "I have a cousin two years younger than I. She's American. She grew up in Boston, but not in the same . . . comfortable circumstances my brother and I grew up with. I wrote and made her an offer. I would provide a substantial dowry, if she would come and masquerade as my betrothed for the season."

Surprise lit Hestia's lovely face. "How . . . logical of you."

"It's the perfect idea," he insisted. "A few months spent here, then she could return home to attract a whole different class of suitor with an appropriate dowry behind her. And in the meantime, I would feel . . . free."

"Free to do what?" Hestia asked gently.

He thought about it. "Free to move about Town without constant tension. Free to continue to find my way into this role. And yes, free to meet people without worrying about their motives. I know my duty, Hestia. I will marry someday, but it will be a day of my own choosing, and not to someone who hunts me down like a dog with a bone, only so that she can live in a fairy tale castle."

"I gather, since you are here, that your cousin did not agree?"

"On the contrary, she did agree. I booked her passage here and thought to meet her ship yesterday." He sighed again. "But she was not aboard and the captain only had a letter saying that a beau stepped up at the last minute and convinced her that she didn't need a dowry or a voyage to England."

"And now?"

"You know what I mean to ask. I can see it in your face. I want to find a young lady to take my cousin's place."

"Good heavens."

"Yes, I know."

Hestia looked thoughtful. "It will take a very particular sort of girl to fill this position."

"I'm aware of that. She must be a gentlewoman—or be able to pass as one."

"She must be somewhat desperate herself, to agree to such a thing," Hestia added.

"True. And she cannot wish to mix in Society after this Season, because once we have finished with this masquerade, I will put it about that my cousin decided that we did not suit and returned to America."

Hestia tapped her fingertips together. "Where will this paragon stay while she pretends to be your cousin?"

"At Herrington House—with my mother. I won't be staying there. Hell and damnation, at this point I'd be safer in Seven Dials. But I'll find bachelor's rooms or put up at a hotel."

"Your *mother* has agreed to go along with this scheme?"

"She had already agreed to go along with Emmaline's masquerade. I rather think she meant to promote the match and make it a reality. But after this morning, she will go along with whatever I put into motion."

"Well, then. You've everything in hand, do you not?"

"Except for finding the right girl."

"Do you know, my lord, there is a chance that she might be closer than you think." She leaned forward and reached up, opening a small panel that allowed her to speak to the coachman. "Slow down, just a bit, will you please?" she called. "Traffic is light enough, it should not cause a problem. Have you caught sight of the girl? She's just ahead, moving toward the Cumberland gate."

Hart didn't hear the driver answer, but Hestia must have been satisfied. She sat back and watched out the window. "Now, you just sit back and let me work, my lord." She met his gaze directly. "And kindly recall your promise. Do not interfere, unless I ask you to."

***

Emily watched the family ahead closely. Her brothers and sister romped around Miss

Carmichael, excited to be so close to the freedom of the park. The girl laughed with them and with their nurse. She was dressed in another overdone gown. Emily looked forward to seeing her in something that would highlight her fresh looks instead of burying them.

She would instigate a meeting with the girl even if she had to trip over one of her frightful flounces. She would instigate a conversation about fashions and offer to introduce her to a talented modiste, one still largely undiscovered and therefore economical. Madame Lalbert was ready, armed with a nearly complete day dress for the girl to try, and a selection of simple and elegant designs that would make her stand out in the right way . . . and Emily would receive a percentage of the profits from the order.

She could almost feel the comforting weight of the coins in her pocketbook. She would stop at a cook shop and purchase a thick, meaty stew for dinner—something to tempt Mama and fill Jasper up. Perhaps a loaf—

"Miss Carmichael is a lovely girl. I hope you intend to treat her in a kinder fashion than you did Miss Paxton."

Emily froze—and turned to find a breathtakingly beautiful lady coming up behind her—amusement shining in her blue eyes.

"Excuse me?" Her heart was trying to pound right out of her chest.

'I've no quarrel with how you duped Miss Paxton. That one deserves to be taken down a peg or two. But Miss Carmichael is by all reports a sweet, innocent girl."

"She does seem so," Emily agreed. She felt very queer indeed—and she could not tear her eyes from the woman who stared back at her with a mix of approval and curiosity. "Who *are* you? How did you know—"

"About Miss Paxton?" The woman smiled, cat-like. "I am Hestia Wright, my dear. I know a great deal of what happens in London, and I am able to find out the rest, when I am interested." She reached out and linked her arm through Emily's. "Come. Let us walk a bit, for I am *very* interested in you."

"Why?" Then it struck her. Hestia Wright. The famed former courtesan, owner of Half Moon House, a safe place where any woman could come for help, with anything . . .

"Ah, there it is," Hestia murmured. "I assume you are in a bind? In need of funds?"

Emily nodded, her mind working frantically.

"Did you not think to come to me?"

"No!" She should have. It hadn't occurred to her. She'd thought the women who approached Hestia Wright were those in truly dire circumstances or mortal danger . . .

"Well, I can see the wheels turning now. And I may be in a position to help you, my dear, if you will but answer a few questions."

Emily nodded, still not quite recovered from her shock.

"Your name is Emily Spencer?"

"Yes, ma'am."

"Just Hestia, if you please. "And what *do* you intend to do with Miss Carmichael?"

She explained.

Hestia looked pleased at the end of it. "Inventive. But I imagine her mother would be a blocking point. How will you convince her to consider the purchase of a new wardrobe?"

"I wrote her mother an anonymous note, stating that polite Society was not being so polite about her daughter's overblown, outdated, countrified fashions."

"Inventive," Hestia said approvingly. "She won't like that. And you have the good judgment to use a light touch."

"Not so light," Emily admitted. "I did make the arrangement with Madame ahead of time."

"Good planning will not make me think any less of you, my dear. But tell me, do you not have any family? No one to turn to, instead of going to such efforts?"

"No." Emily hesitated. "Not *real* family—and not anyone I would trust to have our best interests at heart."

Hestia Wright regarded her thoughtfully, and the moment stretched out. The Carmichaels turned into the park, and Emily made the choice to continue strolling with Hestia while she mulled her situation over.

"Very well," Hestia said at last. "The situation I have in mind is . . . peculiar. But you are the right age and well-spoken." She paused. "You can read?"

"Of course!" She spoke dourly. "And my mathematics are up to par, as well."

Hestia laughed. "Can you dance, by any chance?"

"Dance?" Now that one startled her. "Not really, beyond a few country dances."

"Well, that could be explained away. Do Americans dance, after all? I don't really know."

"Americans?" Emily's mind started to race. "Is this a position that you speak of? I'm not sure I could take a position . . . depending on the circumstances and definitely not if it required me to move away. I could not leave and abandon my . . . obligations."

"It is a temporary position only, my dear, and right here in London. But it would require you to relocate for a few weeks. Do you think that your obligations could do without you for a few weeks? You would be well compensated for your trouble."

Emily thought a moment. "Perhaps. If I could be advanced part of that compensation."

"I'm sure that could be arranged." Hestia leaned in close. "It is a strange situation, there is no doubt. But it might be just what you need. There is a peer of the realm, you see, and he is in dire circumstances . . ."

Chapter Three

Was that the girl she had in mind? The one to play his betrothed? Hart did as Hestia bade him and stayed in the carriage, but he craned his neck, trying to see. He'd caught only a glimpse of the girl before Hestia moved her off ahead of the carriage. He'd noticed only an oversized pelisse and a smart little bonnet. Now, straining, he could only make out a plain gown peeking out from underneath her outerwear— and that she talked with great animation. They stayed, conversing for several minutes before Hestia turned and headed back toward the coach, bringing the girl with her.

He sat back, on edge now that the moment was at hand. But he would find a way to be left in peace. And he was wild with curiosity to see the girl Hestia thought would do for his unusual request.

The coachman climbed down and moved to open the door. Still talking over her shoulder to Hestia, the girl climbed in first. She sounded full of energy and anticipation, and then she turned her head. She caught sight of him, waiting there—and froze.

His breath caught.

She was . . . unexpected. The noise from the street, the hustle of pedestrians on the pavement, they all faded away. There was only a pair of large grey eyes in a sweet, heart-shaped face.

Porcelain skin and a generous pink mouth. Pursed in mid-word, that wide mouth caught his attention and held him fast.

"You're it?" she rasped. Clearing her throat, she tried again. "You're him, I mean?"

"Please sit, my dear." Hestia Wright sounded amused. "So that I may answer your question and address more than the back of your skirt."

Color rose over those intriguing cheekbones. She looked chagrined as she entered the rest of the way into the carriage and took the opposite seat. Another glance at him and she sent Hestia a disbelieving look. "That's him? The peer that needs a pretend fiancé?"

"It is he, indeed. My lord, may I present Miss Emily Spencer? Emily, the Earl of Hartford."

"An earl. An *earl* wants me to masquerade as his betrothed?"

"I gave her only the barest details," Hestia said to him. "The rest will better come from you." She looked back and motioned the coachman back up into his perch. "Watkins, take them to . . . ." She paused and looked at the girl. "It was Cheapside, was it not?"

At her nod, she continued her orders to the driver. "Off to Cheapside with you, and leave Miss Spencer wherever she likes. Then drop his lordship at home before you return."

"Wait." The girl looked suddenly panicked. "Are you not coming along?"

"Is that wise?" Hart asked.

"This is best hammered out privately, between the two of you." She met Hart's gaze directly. "I believe that Emily is just the girl to accomplish your task beautifully." She turned to the girl. "Miss Spencer, Lord Hartford is a gentleman in every sense of the word. I put you into his hands knowing he will treat you like the gentlewoman you are."

She closed the door and smiled at them through the open window. "Now, I believe I will call on a friend. I will expect to hear from you this afternoon, my lord. You will let me know whether the pair of you can come to an agreement or not."

Hart agreed. Hestia signaled the driver, and they were off. He found himself sitting across from a stranger—and staring again.

She stared right back, her face ablaze with nerves, curiosity—and skepticism. Oddly enough, it was that wariness that struck a chord of empathy in him. He knew how it felt to wonder if you could trust the company you found yourself in.

Perhaps she was the right girl for the job.

She sucked in a breath and held it for a moment. Slowly, she exhaled. "Well then. Let's have the worst of it out first, shall we?" Meeting his gaze directly she asked, "What exactly, is wrong with you, my lord?"

Then again, she might not be the one he was looking for.

"What?" He recoiled slightly. "There is nothing wrong with me."

"Come now. A title, the money to go with it, I presume, and that face?" She gestured. "And still you need to hire a fiancée? Either there is something wrong with you or something has gone collectively wrong with the young ladies of the *ton*."

Indignation faded. "Ah. You've hit it on the head—but struck the wrong nail. I am fine. The young ladies of the ton, however, are a brassy lot. They are not *reluctant* to consider me, instead they are far too eager, too bold and too numerous."

"Oh," she sat back. "I'm to shield you from them, then?"

She had a quick mind, at least. "Yes," he said with relief.

"You are under siege, so to speak."

"Exactly."

She gave a little laugh and shook her head.

"It's far from amusing, I assure you."

"I'm not laughing at you, I promise." She shook her head. "I am only imagining what my Scottish grandmother would say at this." Her grin stretched wide and he was caught, unused to a girl who showed real emotion instead of polite tittering and ennui. "She was full of those delightful old witticisms, like 'a nod's as good as a wink tae a blind horse!'"

"My grandmother never said as much to me," he said lightly, "but I suppose it's true enough."

"She'd have plenty to say about this. She'd accuse you of trying to pass a sow's ear off as a silk purse."

He bit back a laugh. "Miss Spencer, we may only have the shortest acquaintance, but I assure you, you have many more charms that a sow's ear."

"I thank you," she said with a nod. "Now me . . ." She sighed and grew more sober. "She might tell me that if you've something to hide, the safest place is under someone's nose."

He stilled. "Are you hiding something, Miss Spencer?"

She blinked at him, and then grinned again. "Only my nerves, I hope. I admit I find myself tempted by the job, my lord, and amused by the irony of fate, bringing us together. We could not be more opposite, you see. You have too much interest in your situation. I, on the other hand, would feel infinitely richer for the favorable interest of just one person." Her mouth twitched. "I don't count the interest of a landlord chasing me down for rent, you see, or a butcher who is only interested in trading favors for finer cuts of meat."

Good God. Well. At least she needed him as much as he needed her.

"Too bad we couldn't just make a trade between us," she said with a smile. "But here we are instead, on the verge of a perilous pretense."

"Perilous?" Hart frowned. Why did he feel slightly bewildered every time she spoke? "Daunting perhaps. It will be quite a bit of work, especially for you. But perilous?"

"Daunting for me, perhaps you are right." Her gaze unfocused as if she were thinking.

"There are obstacles. I don't have the right wardrobe, for one."

"I'll see to that," he said easily.

"And will I not need a sponsor, if you wish me to go about in Society?" She frowned. "I assume you do wish me to make public appearances, otherwise why bother?"

"My mother will be your sponsor."

She blinked. "Truly? Well, that will solve a whole host of difficulties, I should think. But still, this is a perilous business for you, my lord."

"For me?" She'd stumped him again.

"Yes, for you will be quite at my mercy, won't you?" She shook her head. "Hestia Wright was wrong about one thing—I'm not a gentlewoman, not really."

He had no idea how to respond to that.

"I have ties to your *beau monde*, if I am to be truthful."

"Truthful would be best," he agreed ironically.

"Actually, my mother has ties—to some of the highest blood in the land. But they are not *recognized* ties, if you know what I mean."

Did he? She was illegitimately connected to Society? And would it interfere?

Frowning greatly, she appeared to be considering the same question. "But my situation is not likely to change and I do not have to use my real name—which likely means nothing to anyone, anyway." She nodded, as if she'd solved the puzzle to her satisfaction. "There now. We can forge ahead. And you can rest assured that you are in good hands, my lord. There are a great many unscrupulous girls in every class of society. I can imagine any one of them who would go along with your scheme, just for a chance to cry foul and compromise later—and force your hand. Never mind that the betrothal was false, the marriage would be real enough—or your honor destroyed."

Hart stilled, but she merely smiled and forged on. "It's a good thing you found me, then, isn't it? I'll never play you false like that, sir. I'll stick strictly to the terms of our agreement."

She raised her brows expectantly.

He was still reeling from her little speech. What a fascinating conundrum she was. Clearly she'd had a little experience with the wicked ways of the world, but next to none with persons in his position. If he toyed with a girl of his own class, he would be caught, as she said. But with her—a girl with no family, no protection? She was in more danger from him than the reverse. Did she not know that he could have her jailed with a word? He could easily crush her future, and the future of anyone else who lived with her in Cheapside.

But he would not. He was a man of his word—and a man a bit unbalanced by her charming mix of worldliness and naïveté.

Or perhaps the sensation was caused by the odd motion of her brows, still dancing up and down as she gazed at him, waiting.

For what? "Errr...?' Thank God there was no one here to witness the utter defeat of his sangfroid.

"The terms?" she repeated. "Of our agreement?"

"Oh, yes. Much of the groundwork is laid," he told her. "I'd been expecting my cousin to play the role, you see. A distant cousin, from America."

"Ah, that's where the Americans come in." She frowned. "*Do* they dance?"

He gaped at her. "I don't know." But the thought struck him. "Do you?"

"Barely," she admitted.

"Well, we can have a dancing instructor in. I've no doubt you will pick it up quickly." He cast a dark look at her ensemble. "I assume you are sound, under all of that."

She laughed. "Sound enough to dance at a few balls. And you may laugh if you like, but this outfit is as good as armor."

"Armor?"

"Yes. I am making deliveries later today. Ironic, that I'm delivering articles meant to enhance and bring attention to a girl's looks— but the safest bet is to downplay my own. It's best to be invisible, out here on my own. But I'm tall, and that makes it difficult. So I go for dowdy, harried, and hurried."

"I see." He did not like to think of her wandering the streets unprotected. Fortunate again, then, that her waggling eyebrows distracted him again.

"Sir?" she asked. "Can we please address the *terms*?"

"Oh. Yes. I had offered my cousin a respectable dowry in return for her help. I will offer you the same amount, of course."

"A dowry." He rather thought she was holding her breath. "How much?"

"Two thousand pounds."

It was her turn to gape. "Two . . . *thousand . . .* pounds?" she repeated weakly.

He nodded.

She went boneless and leaned back against the seat.

He laughed. "Satisfactory, then? Good. In return, you will stay with my mother through the Season. We'd already decided that we would keep it a quiet stay. No court presentation or large, fancy betrothal ball. We've put it out that Emmaline was not used to going about in Society much, but you will be expected to go along with many of the other usual activities—teas, calls, the occasional ball or night at the theatre, walks in the park, etc."

She stared at him for a moment, then sat straight again. "And us, my lord?"

"Us?"

"What will we do together? As a newly betrothed couple?"

"Oh. Well, I suppose I shall take you for a ride in the park, send you a posy or two. Dance with you when it cannot be helped. That sort of thing. Fortunately it's not fashionable for engaged couples to live in each other's pockets."

"Fortunately," she repeated wryly.

"I daresay you won't see much of me at all."

"If that is what you wish, then it will be as you say," she promised with the air of someone making a vow.

He thought about it. "I suppose I just want you to keep your head down," he mused. "I wish you to be seen but to move quietly through the next few weeks, and I shall do the same, if there is any justice in the world."

She thrust her hand out. "Shall we shake on it, then, my lord?"

He took her small, white hand in his—and was dismayed to feel the calluses on her gloveless fingers.

Oblivious, she continued. "Now, when and how shall I arrive at your home?"

He shook himself back into the present. "I'd like to maintain the illusion that you've come from America, even with the servants. If you could, get yourself to this shipping company's address at ten o'clock tomorrow morning . . ."

* * *

Emily lifted her chin and allowed Madame Lalbert to fuss with the buttons of her new pelisse. The hackney swayed horribly as they navigated the narrow streets of Wapping, but the modiste and her needle persisted. "There," she said at last. "You are ready, and a fine job of it I did too, in just a few hours."

"Thank you, Madame," Emily said fervently.

"It will be well worth it when you come in to order your new wardrobe."

"I will, I promise. And thank you so much for taking Mama in. I'll be so much easier knowing that you are looking out for her and Jasper."

"It will be quite a nice change," her mother piped in. "Madame has asked me to look over her books and help out in the showroom. You know how much I've missed running the shop, my dear. It will be as if I'm having an adventure as you are having yours."

"Yes—and I will be able to see you when I come for selections and fittings—but most importantly, at the end of it we'll have enough money to do as we please." She reached for her hand. "How does a little ribbon shop in Edinburgh sound, Mama? You've talked of going home again. You could have the run of a smaller enterprise—and only embroider when you wished to."

"Oh!" Her mother's eyes shone. "Isn't that a fine idea?"

"Don't s'pose you'll need a delivery boy?" Jasper interjected.

"Oh, no." Meeting her mother's eye, Emily shook her head. "We'll be looking for a fine young apprentice, though, to learn the running of the business."

"Me?"

"Who else?"

Jasper swelled with pride.

"Emily, it sounds grand, but are you sure—"

"I'm sure, Mama." Emily refused to think otherwise.

"I want you to be careful," her mother said, her tone going low and urgent. "Enjoy yourself as you can, but remember that this is only temporary. I don't want you to grow too used to such a fine lifestyle—or for such company—and pine for it when it's gone."

Her heart softened. Emily knew what went unspoken beneath her mother's words. Quiet longing for someone who was never coming—Emily knew what that looked like, because she'd seen it in her mother's face over the years. "Don't fret," she reassured her. "Lord Hartsford is a gentleman and will treat me fairly. And I am harboring no girlish dreams of becoming a countess. I have promised to adhere to the letter of our agreement and so I shall." She smiled gently. "It's a business arrangement, nothing more."

"Of course."

"Here is where we'll stop," Madame Lalbert said, looking out the window. "Jasper, you see her safely to the warehouse, then stay close and watch over her until his lordship arrives. Come straight back, then. We'll wait for you." She handed Emily her portmanteau. "We'll expect you to be a frequent visitor at the shop."

"I feel a veritable mania for fashion coming on," Emily laughed. "Goodbye, Mama." She kissed her soft cheek. "I will see you very soon."

"Take care, my dear," her mother whispered. "Please, take care."

Emily kissed her again and descended from the coach. She had to fight back tears as she and Jasper set off, but it grew easier as they moved away. She could do this. She was happy to do this and secure a better future for them all.

"What if he sees you, Em?" Jasper looked worried. "The old gentleman? What if he sees you at one of them balls?"

"That's the beauty of it, Jasper. Even if the old Duke spots me across a ballroom, he won't *see* me. He's looking for a girl in the street, not just another debutante. The girl he's looking for dresses in shapeless sacks and covers her hair with a cheap scarf. Instead, I'll be dressed in pastels, one more young miss in a sea of them. It's the perfect place to hide!"

"If you say so." He didn't seem convinced. "He doesn't seem like a dim one to me."

"Well, he was never bright enough to wish to recognize Mama as one of his own, so I don't set great store by his judgment." And that was irrefutable, in her opinion. Anyone who ignored the chance to be a part of her mother's life was foolish beyond redemption.

Jasper gave in as they grew near the shipping office. Emily gave his hand a quick squeeze, and entered. The clerk in the front room merely shrugged when she asked if she might wait for his lordship, before going back to his work. Emily took up a position at the window to wait—but it was only minutes before the earl drew up in a gorgeous, lacquered landeau.

She watched him climb down, mutely delighted that she could feast her eyes for a moment, unnoticed.

He was handsome. She'd discovered that in the carriage yesterday. She'd gone to her bed late and her last conscious thought had been of his brown eyes and how they had looked fathoms deep in the dim light, of the chiseled jaw and the proud nose, a shade too long—just long enough to be interesting, not enough to ruin his pleasing profile.

He looked different today, she noticed as he paused for a word with the servant who climbed down from behind. Polished.

Yesterday he'd been the slightest bit disheveled—his hair mussed and his neck cloth crooked and his eyebrows slightly wild and askew. Testimony, she supposed, to the level of agitation he'd been driven to.

Today, though, he looked . . . like an earl. Carved from years of privilege. Consequence and history stretched out behind him and eased his way ahead. He moved into the shop with smooth grace and utter confidence.

She must remember that.

The clerk scrambled to his feet. Hartford gave him a nod, but his gaze fixed on her . . . in surprise and pleasure.

She knew she looked good. Madame Lalbert and her mother had outdone themselves. Her white poplin was trimmed in the same deep smoky blue of her levantine pelisse. It brought out the color in her eyes. The single lace flounce at the bottom and the fancy silk trimming helped transform her from a plain seamstress and sometime delivery girl into someone who could be an elegant young miss.

"There you are, my dear, safely delivered at last." He came forward and bowed low over her hand.

She gave a very creditable curtsy. "My lord. It is so good to see you again."

He took up the portmanteau and handed it off to the servant, who had followed him in.

"I've only the one bag, you see—"

"It's all right. I spoke with Captain Randolph already. He told me of the trouble you all experienced." Playing off her blank look he continued. "I know, it's shocking that he and the *Liberty Belle* made it into port before you, but they limped in yesterday. He had your trunk, but I'm afraid everything inside was quite spoilt."

She did her best to look dismayed.

"Ah, well. It only means you must replenish your wardrobe here in London." He bent a smile upon her. "Mother is already making lists and mapping out trips to modistes and glovers and milliners."

"How kind." She stifled a shiver. She could do this, she knew she could—but his mother could make it easier or harder, depending on her inclination.

"Come. She's anxiously awaiting you."

He offered his arm and Emily took it, thrilling at the warmth of him—and reveling in his height. She couldn't have been sure yesterday, seated as they had been in the carriage, but he stood several inches taller than her. She had to look up to meet his gaze as he pulled her close—and she found it unexpectedly thrilling.

He paused at the door and glanced at the clerk. "I'm sorry to have come when Mr. Wilsden was busy. Tell your employer that I greatly appreciate the use of his office, and the safe spot for my betrothed to await me." He ignored the man's surprise, cast a fond look down on her and ushered her outside.

He bent close. "Now, let the news begin to circulate—it will start here and soon be everywhere in Town," he said with a smirk. He motioned for the footman to take a seat with the driver instead of behind, then handed her into the forward facing seat. "I thought you might wish to see the city," he said. "So I had them open the carriage."

He sat next to her and it felt . . . exotic and strange and warm. "Thank you," she breathed. It wasn't difficult for her to feign wide-eyed and intimidated. "It's very large, isn't it?"

"A good deal larger than Boston." He lowered his tone. "We should be able to have some private conversation and allow the world to see you at the same time," he said. "Two birds with one stone."

"Admirably logical of you, my lord."

"The sooner the females of the *ton* learn of your existence, the quicker I get my life back." He let his gaze roam over her and she tried not to enjoy the approval he radiated. "I did not expect to find you looking so . . . well."

It felt good to surprise him. "I'm not entirely without resources, sir." Her mouth quirked. "Just mostly."

From this angle, and from so close a vantage, she looked up into a marvelous visage of sun-hewn angles and shadowed valleys. It was quite as inspiring as the gorgeous vistas in her mother's Highland home.

Playing his part, he raised his voice. He spoke of the wealth of a nation that made its way through this busy riverside district and eventually swept his hand toward the thoroughfare ahead. "We're coming up to the Strand, cousin. I doubt you have such long and busy streets at home, eh?"

She shook her head, grateful for pretense their mission provided and for the noise of the increased traffic as they made their turn. "Perhaps this is a good time for you to tell me what I need to know about your cousin?"

"What do you need to know?" he asked.

His tone had gone absent-sounding and she glanced over to find his gaze was not on the traffic around them, but on the trim that chased the buttons down the front of her coat—and over her curves.

"Her name?" she suggested flatly. "You mentioned the name Emmaline yesterday? Do you think we could shorten it to Emily? It might make things easier."

"I don't see why not. She is Emmaline Latham." He paused. "And I suppose you should call me Hart. Everyone who is close to me does."

"I will too, then," she said, trying to sound business-like. "What else can you tell me about her?"

"Let me think. She is—no, *you* are my first cousin. Your mother is my mother's youngest sister. She fell in love with a Navy captain, and followed him to America when he sold out and went to Boston to build ships. My aunt, your mother, died of a fever years ago."

"How old was I?"

"About ten, I believe."

She nodded, absorbing the information. "Do I get along with my father?"

He grimaced. "I haven't the foggiest notion."

"I think that I do," she decided. "Perhaps I will miss him dreadfully and long to return to him."

"Oh, yes. Good thinking."

"What are her passions and pursuits?"

He looked ashamed. "I don't know that either." His brows rose. "What are yours?"

She hesitated—and then decided to be candid. "To be honest, sir, my main pursuit is in search of rent money."

"Oh. Of course. I'm sorry to be insensitive."

"Not at all. I just wanted to be forthright with you. I am a seamstress, mainly. I take in piecework from modistes who are busy enough to hire out. My—" She paused, not sure just how open she needed to be. "I also help with and deliver fine embroidered pieces and ribbons."

"While trying to stay invisible," he said softly.

"In a nutshell," she said cheerily. "Now, what are your interests, my lord? What do you do when you are not hiring a fiancé off of the streets?"

Laughing a little, he rubbed his brow. "Oddly enough, I spend my time in a somewhat similar fashion. At least, trying to make several estates pay for themselves instead of draining the family coffers often feels like scrambling to make rent."

She doubted he'd ever gone hungry in search of his goal, but she refrained from saying so.

He raised his voice again, then, and pointed out Charing Cross, the parks and other points of interest. Emily sat, nodding, murmuring and enjoying the timbre of his voice. They moved into the west end of town and several times he nodded to acquaintances in passing vehicles. She also caught pedestrians staring as they rode by.

He seemed well pleased by it. "Word will start going around right away. Not even home yet, and we've made a good start." He leaned in. "While I have the chance, I wish to thank you, and tell you I'll do what I can to help. Are you feeling confident about all of this?

She was feeling that her mother was right; she was going to have to be careful. Even knowing his solicitous attention was false, she was still enjoying it.

"Honestly, it seems little enough for me to do," she admitted. "This must be a change for you, though, to be courting attention, instead of avoiding it."

He shrugged. "It feels damned good to think of putting gossip to work *for* me, for once." He frowned. "Do not mistake me, though. Your existence as my betrothed is all the notoriety I need. Ideally, we need to strike a balance. Make you known, without calling too much attention to us."

She nodded. "I understand."

"It should be simple enough. All you need to do is be quiet and polite and follow my mother's lead."

She tried to shrug off a wave of irritation. "I know how to behave, my lord," she said sourly. "My mother had a lady's education—and she saw me taught as well. I won't be tossing my skirts over my head, running down St. James' or chasing the young bucks of the *ton*."

"Of course not. I apologize." But he sounded relieved rather than sorry. "Ah, here we go," he said as they turned into Portman Square.

She sighed audibly at the sight of the wide streets, the grand houses and the oval garden in the center.

"Here's Herrington House." The landau pulled to a stop. He smiled as she gazed up, drinking in the sight. "It really is a lovely home—one of the best things to come with the title, in my opinion." He climbed down and turned to hold out a hand to assist her. "Of course, it isn't the jeweled crown that is Hartsworth . . .

She took his hand, her gaze fixed on the house. She was intimidated just by all of the windows sparkling at her—all four stories of them. Could she convince the world that she belonged here? "A jeweled crown," she shuddered, trying not to let her nerves show. "Do tell me I won't have to wear it."

"Wear it?" He sounded confused. "Wear what?"

"The jeweled crown. What did you call it?" She shivered again and climbed down. "Is it so important that it has its own name?"

"Hartsworth." His grip tightened suddenly, crushing her fingers.

She tried to retrieve her hand, but he held on. "Truly, sir, I've no wish for you to haul out the family jewels for my sake. It's too much responsibility."

He still had not let her go. "Is it so important, then?" she asked. "Must I be seen in it?"

He looked dazed. "No."

She tugged again and he realized what he was doing. Abruptly, he let her go.

"Good." She rubbed at her hand.

He stared at her again, but something about the way he looked at her had changed. It was a look full of assessment . . . and warmth. The air prickled between them again.

She thought, suddenly, that it was a very good thing that they weren't going to see much of each other during this masquerade.

"Let's go in," he said suddenly. "Are you ready?"

She swallowed. And nodded. "Ready."

Chapter Four

He'd been feeling so fine and full of himself. He'd done it. Or Hestia Wright had. She'd found the girl who was going to save him from the nightmare of constant pursuit.

He'd thought the hard part over. The rest would be easy. All he had to do now was to let his mother take over, pay not-too-much attention to the girl and go about his business.

Except . . .

He hadn't expected her to look so . . . different. She'd stepped toward him out of the gloom of that office this morning—and it had been like the sun coming up. She'd looked so tall and slender—and unexpectedly curvy. He'd swallowed. No wonder she'd worn that sack-like gown before. Without it, she'd be prey to random men in the streets and their eye for a voluptuous figure.

Hell—she'd be subject to the same from the men of the ton, without his protection. Especially with the way that pelisse hugged her curves and how the misty blue of it made her eyes look like the sky after a rain.

She hadn't been self-conscious about the change, either. Rather, she'd been easy in his company. Honest and funny and not awed by the difference in their circumstances.

And she'd never heard of Hartsworth.

The shock of it still held him in sway. The prospect was so fresh and new and entirely unexpected that he felt the need to express it again.

She'd never heard of Hartsworth.

Since his earliest memory it seemed as if he'd been defined by the notoriety of his home and family. When he met someone, even as a boy, he'd seen the knowledge in their eyes, felt the weight of their expectations. He was a Herrington. He'd grown up in a castle, for heaven's sake. Everyone looked at him and thought his life would be charmed. His path would be easy. His pockets would be full and his marriage would be a grand love match, blissful in every way.

And ever since he'd first realized that this was his heritage, this was what people saw when they looked at him; he'd half-worried, half-wondered.

What would happen if he bollixed it all up?

"The Countess is in the parlor, my lord," the butler intoned.

"Thank you, Bridges."

Hart waited while Emily was divested of her outerwear. He nearly cursed when he saw that the day gown beneath showcased her figure even more than the fitted pelisse. He tore his eyes away and looked up instead as she lifted off her bonnet. Her hair was ebony, as he'd glimpsed yesterday, and gathered up into a neat and elegant twist. Why then, must he fight off an image of his fingers picking it apart, pin by pin? Would it curl when it fell or would it fall straight and heavy to her—

He shook his head. She was smiling at someone. He turned his head and saw one of the maids peeking from the library, hoping for a glimpse of the next countess, no doubt. The girl caught him watching, gasped, and ducked back inside.

Emily pursed her lips.

"There you are, darling." His mother beckoned him from the parlor.

He moved away to greet her, kissed her on the cheek and put his lips near her ear. "She's never heard of Hartsworth, Mother."

She drew back and glanced over at Emily, who hung back a little, and then back at him.

"I haven't told her," he continued. "I'd prefer if you didn't."

Conflicting emotions crossed her face. Disbelief. Speculation. "She'll find out, Hart. It won't take long."

He nodded. "I know. But I'll enjoy it in the meanwhile."

She pressed her lips together and turned away. "Emmaline, my dear! I'm so glad you've arrived safely! Come in! Goodness, you were but a girl the last time I saw you." She ushered them toward a grouping of chairs. "Bridges, we are not to be disturbed," she called over her shoulder. "Except for the tea tray. Please tell cook that our guest has arrived."

Hart stepped forward as the servant withdrew. "My cousin has undoubtedly grown, Mother, but she has shortened her name. She's asked that we call her Emily now."

"Have you, my dear?" His mother raised a brow at the pair of them. She paused then, just before she took her seat and raised a finger. Crossing quickly to the door, she opened it. Hart gaped at the butler, standing close and clearly eavesdropping.

"I need you to stand at the front window, Bridges," she told him pleasantly. "I'll need a report on the parasols that pass by this morning, and a count by color."

"Very good, madam." Without the slightest loss of dignity he bowed and moved away.

His mother closed the door again. "Nosey servants can be quite useful," she said to Emily, "or an utter nuisance. The trick is to know which . . . and when."

Emily's eyes sparkled, but she merely nodded. "I shall take your word for it, ma'am."

He judged they were safe enough for true introductions, now. "Mother, may I present Miss Emily Spencer? Emily, my mother, the Countess of Hartford."

Curtsies all around, and they sat.

"So, we are truly taking this path?" his mother asked, looking between them.

"It's already begun." He told her of the attention they'd sparked.

She sighed. "Very well, then." She pulled a folded bit of paper from her sleeve. "It's as well that I heard from your uncle, then. We need not fear your cousin changing her mind. She's truly married—to a Quaker. They intend to go to the American frontier to spread the Light to the heathens."

"How noble of her," he murmured. But he had to admit he was relieved.

The countess turned a measuring gaze upon Emily, then.

His false betrothed lifted her chin.

Hart hoped he would not be called to take sides.

A knock sounded and the tea tray came in. He muffled his sigh of relief. The maid set the tray nearby and he noticed that Emily watched her closely. He also noticed his mother noticed—and didn't look approving. Were they going to start off with a lecture already?

When the girl had gone, Emily met his mother's gaze directly. "Would you like me to pour and set your mind at ease?"

The countess raised a brow and waved permission—and then thawed when Emily must have performed the task to some unknown feminine standard.

"Very well, my dear, let us call truce. It is clear you've been trained."

It was clear she awaited an explanation.

Emily took a small sandwich. "As I told his lordship, my mother received a lady's education."

"Is she a lady?" his mother asked sharply.

"No. My grandparents were merchants. They started a successful linen draper's shop and turned it into a large import enterprise." She cleared her throat. "They were not blessed with children of their own, though, after years of marriage."

"Ah." His mother sat back. "They raised a gentleman's child?"

Emily nodded. "My mother. She was educated and she saw me taught as well."

"Whose child is she?"

Emily's chin shot up again. "I have not shared that information with his lordship. It is not my secret to tell."

"It will not interfere in your playing this role?"

"I do not believe so, my lady."

"Very well," his mother relented. Hart thought he caught a glimpse of approval in her eye.

"Word has spread regarding our arrival," his mother said, turning to him. "No more girls falling on the walk, but the invitations are stacked on my desk." She quirked a corner of her mouth at Emily. "When word of *you* gets out, I expect they'll double. We must get you ready."

"I'll engage a dancing instructor," Hart told her. "Just to make sure Emily is current."

They both nodded and the conversation devolved into a discussion of wardrobe, modistes and shopping plans to start as soon as the next day. Hart considered taking his leave, but he delayed when the maid came back for the tray, and kept an eye trained on Emily.

She didn't stare this time, but instead reached out and touched the maid's arm.

His mother made a sound of distress.

The girl gasped and jumped back as if she'd been burned.

"Hello," Emily said in the friendliest fashion. "What is your name?"

The maid cast a frantic look at the countess, then bobbed a curtsy. "I'm Molly, Miss. If you please."

"Please don't look so frightened. I'm sure we'll get to know each other over the next few weeks, but for now I must say that I noticed the swelling of your jaw. Have you a bad tooth?"

Hart gaped as the girl clapped a hand over her face. "Oh! I swear, I haven't complained too much, Miss, nor let it interfere—"

"Of course you haven't," Emily soothed. "I only ask because a friend of mine recently dealt with the same situation. Have you an appointment to have it seen? I assure you, the sooner you have it dealt with, the better."

"Oh, no, Miss. I'm using the cloves that Cook give me. I've only the half day off on Wednesday, you see."

Hart looked closely. He could see the swelling now. It must hurt like the devil. He hadn't noticed before. Would he have? "Of course, you must have it seen to." He looked at his mother. "Surely she could be spared . . ."

His mother wasn't examining the girl, but instead was giving Emily a good, long look. Then she slid her gaze over the maid and smiled gently. "I'm very sorry I didn't notice your distress, Molly. Miss Latham is right, however. The sooner you see to such a problem, the soon you will feel better and the fewer lasting effects you will suffer." She nodded a dismissal. "Take the tray to Cook, then run along to Mrs.

Hanshaw. She'll make you an appointment and will be sure someone will go along with you, too."

The girl dipped once, twice. "Oh, thank you, my lady." She shot Emily a look of adoration. "And thank you, Miss Latham."

Emily nodded cheerfully. "My friend was as right as rain as soon as he had it out. I'm sure you will be, too."

When the maid had gone, Hart watched the two women sizing each other up again.

"I gather that was not what I should have done?" Emily straightened her shoulders. "I apologize, but I did not wish to see the girl suffer—"

"It was well done," his mother interrupted. "I'm only ashamed I did not notice, myself." Unexpectedly, she raised her cup in a mock toast. "To our enterprise," she said with a smile. "I think we will do very well."

Emily visibly relaxed. She raised her own cup and shot him a challenging look. "What of you, sir? Do you feel we'll pull it off to your satisfaction?"

He stared. Earlier he had felt every confidence. But he realized now it was because he'd only been thinking of himself. But this girl—she made it impossible to forget she was part of the equation. More than that. She had spirit, and abundant curves and a kind heart— and an ignorance of Hartsworth—and she held his fate in his hands.

He'd taken too long to answer. Her smile faded and concern and consternation invaded. "If you have doubts," she began.

"No. Forgive me." He raised his cup as well. "I was just thinking that you are unlike any young woman of my acquaintance."

Her shoulders lowered and she tossed him a grin. "I believe that's why you hired me, Hart."

God help him, she was right.

* * *

They were definitely not living in each other's pockets. Emily's last several days had been filled with shopping and planning. She'd grown more comfortable with the earl's mother and managed to sneak in a few moments with her own at Madame Lalbert's shop. But she scarcely caught a glimpse of Hart.

She told herself that she didn't mind. This was the arrangement she'd agreed to. But she found herself listening for his arrival and eagerly anticipating the start of their masquerade.

"Our first foray will be to call on the Marchioness of Feltham," the countess informed her at last. "She's my sister. We haven't seen each other in months, and she's just arrived in Town, so we'll spend the afternoon catching up and receiving callers with her, instead of limiting ourselves to the usual fifteen minutes."

"Will the earl be joining us?" It was just a casual question. She repeated the thought to herself in hopes of believing it this time.

"No. This is exactly the sort of thing he's hoping to avoid," his mother said.

Emily nodded. She was not disappointed, merely nervous.

Perhaps she'd better repeat that one too.

But all went well. The marchioness was kind and welcomed her as if a relation of her sister's husband was a relation of hers. No one questioned her identity for a moment. She smiled and nodded and took tea and pretended interest as Lady Hartsford and her sister gossiped.

Her day brightened when Mrs. Carmichael and her daughter Mary came to call. Emily invited the girl to sit next to her. They had a delightful time getting to know one another and discussing London's public parks and gardens.

"You seem so knowledgeable about the city, Miss Latham," Miss Carmichael remarked. "But didn't you say you'd only just arrived?"

"I spent time here as a child," Emily fibbed. Well, technically it wasn't a lie. She did tell the manufactured tale of her lost wardrobe and described in detail the ball gown that Madame Lalbert and her mother were laboring over—and she invited the girl to come along for her first fitting. She would get the girl into a more flattering wardrobe yet.

The Carmichaels departed, however, and Emily grew bored. An old acquaintance had arrived next and the sisters were busy reminiscing with her. Unnoticed, Emily stood and walked about the room. She stopped at the set of French doors that led to a small terrace. The marquess' home was one of London's few freestanding mansions, which meant it had a substantial garden by city standards. Emily gazed out upon the beauty of it and marveled at the luxury.

It took her a few minutes to notice him. A young gentleman, barely more than a boy, sat in the shade. He looked pale and wan. He held a book in his lap, but stared dejectedly out at the garden instead of reading.

Emily glanced back. The women were deep in childhood memories. She slipped out. Approaching, she peered over his shoulder at the book he held.

"*The Lady of the Lake*," she said. "I did enjoy that one. Made me long to visit Loch Katrine."

The boy started. "Who are you?" he barked over his shoulder. Then he turned back. "Never mind. Just go away."

She noted that one of his arms lay close to his side and the hand and fingers were scarred and twisted.

"Not in the mood for company?" she asked cheerily.

"No."

"Are you ever?"

"No!" he barked.

"Is it a temporary condition, then?"

His head whipped around. "Is *what* a temporary condition?"

"Your bad temper."

His mouth worked, but it was clear he had no idea how to answer—and every desire to lash out in an even more ill-tempered fashion.

"Don't waste your time," she advised. "I'm practically immune to the rudeness of young men. I've one about your age at home."

"Who *are* you?" he bit through gritted teeth.

"Do you really wish to know this time?"

"I really wish to know," he affirmed. "So that I know who I may correctly call the most annoying girl of my acquaintance."

"Bravo—that set-down was well done. But I've hardly reached annoying yet." Crouching down beside him she looked pointedly at his arm. "How did it happen?"

"Don't you know?" He looked surprised.

"How should I? We haven't even met."

"Are you not one of *them*?" He nodded toward the house. "One of the *ton*?"

"Goodness, no!" She laughed. "I'm . . . American."

"Truly?' He sat straighter. "Which part?"

"Boston."

"Oh." He sounded disappointed. "Too civilized for Red Indians, I suppose."

"I know a thing or two about them," Emily hedged.

"Like what?"

"Their skin is not really red, for one. And they dress in buckskins and wear feathers in their hair." She'd heard as much and more from Jasper.

"How I'd like to travel and see them for myself." He sounded despondent.

"It won't be long before you are old enough," she said placatingly.

He glared at her. "Are you blind? Or mad?"

"Neither," she said with a shrug. "Nor are you, from what I can tell."

"I'm crippled," he spat. Struggling, he lifted his arm. "Look at this thing. It is crooked, withered, useless since the accident."

"Are your feet compromised as well?" she said, suddenly stricken.

"No." He frowned.

"Your legs?"

"No."

Emily frowned back at him, thinking. "Were you cack-handed, then?"

"Was I . . . what?"

"Oh, pardon. It's what my Scottish . . . neighbor . . . used to say. Was your left hand dominant—before?"

"No."

Exasperation surged. She let him see it, as she suspected he'd been coddled much of late. "Then why not go to Boston? You don't need that arm to walk aboard a ship."

"I can't swim." Anger surged red in his face.

"It's not required," she said cheekily. "Your ticket covers the whole trip across the Atlantic."

"Why are you talking to me this way?" he asked in a sudden whisper.

"In what way? As if you've a brain and three limbs left?"

"How dare you!" He stood. "I am the heir to the Marquess of Feltham."

"And I am merely Miss Emily Latham, but I know it is absurd to sit here and brood over the things you cannot do rather than be thankful for those you can."

"I can't bowl or bat," he said plaintively. "I was a rollicking good bowler."

"Ah." Emily was all sympathy now. "That is a blow." She frowned. "Move your fingers," she said, pointing.

He stared, but wiggled the fingers on his bad hand.

"Can you grip?"

"Barely."

"Well, then!" she said triumphantly. "Strengthen those muscles and you'll likely ride again. And in the meantime you can write and draw—even fence."

"Fence?" He brightened.

"Well, they only use one hand to hold a foil, do they not?"

He blinked. "I hadn't thought of fencing. The balance . . ." his voice trailed off.

"Can be adjusted for, I'd wager. Give it a try?" A pile of gnarled branches lay next to an apple tree. She took up two and handed him one—and then brandished hers. "Have at me," she said on a laugh.

He stared at her and the branch in his good hand for a moment, then slowly smiled. Standing, he thrust it at her. "*En garde*," he said.

She laughed and smacked his branch with her own . . . and they were off.

Chapter Five

His plan was working perfectly. The rumors of Hart's betrothal flew through the *ton*—and everyone's attention shifted toward his unknown fiancé. Disappointed debutantes abandoned him and concentrated on catching a glimpse of her. Instead of spying out Parliamentary schedules, they stalked the shops of Bond Street, left cards and delivered invitations to Herrington House.

Hart was left to his committees, the business of the earldom and his agricultural interests— exactly the way he'd wanted.

Why then, did he feel this vague dissatisfaction? Why did his brain constantly wander off topic to wonder how she was adjusting, who she was meeting, what she was wearing? Why was his head not filled with plans for abundant fields instead of images of abundant curves?

He didn't know, any more than he knew why his feet were carrying him towards Herrington House this afternoon instead of toward his club where he could search out his friend Peter Grant so he could find out what he'd missed at that lecture the other day.

And yet, here he was, arriving at his own doorstep and being informed that his mother was not at home just as if he was a visitor and not The Earl.

"I'm here to fetch some papers from the study, Bridges," he said testily. "Get out of the way."

He pushed past and took his time finding just what he didn't really need in the first place, but after thirty minutes his mother and Emily had still not returned. Sighing, he gathered up some papers.

"Tell Mother I called," he began to tell Bridges, then stopped. "On second thought, where did they venture off to this afternoon?"

"The countess has asked me not to share her schedule, my lord."

"She didn't mean with me, man!" Hart exclaimed.

The butler raised a brow.

"Who do you think pays your salary, in any case?"

The man's hesitation evaporated. "She's at her sister's, Lady Feltham's."

"Thank you," Hart said with a good dose of sarcasm, as Bridges opened the door. "I've been meaning to head over to see young James, in any case."

He stopped suddenly, as a trio of ladies stood waiting on the stoop.

"Oh, forgive me. Mrs. Paxton, is it not?"

"Indeed." The older lady curtsied. "How kind of you to remember. And this is my daughter, Miss Paxton."

"Miss Paxton," he inclined his head. The third girl was dressed in a more plain fashion and not introduced, so he assumed she must be a maid. "So sorry, ladies, but my mother is not at home and I am on my way out."

"Of course, my lord." Miss Paxton cast him a questioning look. "And are we to offer you felicitations on your engagement, sir? The rumors say as much."

"Ah, yes." It felt different to tell the lie himself. "Well, there's been no announcement yet, but yes." He pushed past. "If you'll excuse me? Good day."

They exchanged glances. "Good day, my lord."

Almost before he knew it, he found himself being welcomed into his aunt's parlor. His mother was there, and another lady, but there was no sign of Emily. He sat, allowed tea to be pressed upon him, but before he could ask after her whereabouts, the door opened again and the Paxtons entered.

Had they followed him? He suppressed a surge of annoyance.

"Oh, how funny to find you again so soon, my lord!" The elder Paxton told the whopper without a flinch.

Another flurry of introductions and Mrs. Paxton joined the ladies while her daughter wandered toward the window.

Finally, Hart had the chance to lean in towards his mother. "Where is Emily? Are you not taking her about with you?"

"Of course!" His mother glanced around. "She is here, somewhere . . ."

"Emily?" his aunt asked. "I thought I saw her step onto the terrace."

"I believe this must be her." Miss Paxton sounded like she was biting back laughter—and not the friendly kind. "Out in the garden."

Hart rose to join her—and swallowed a groan. His faux fiancé was indeed out in the garden, sparring with his young cousin with a set of sticks.

"Perhaps social calls are conducted differently in America," Miss Paxton said snidely. "I did hear that she comes from the colonies?"

"What is it?" his aunt called.

"It is Emily—she's . . . getting to know James," he replied.

"Oh, dear." His aunt rose to join them. "James is quite ill-tempered just now and doesn't want company."

"Well, you did say that your betrothal was not official, my lord," said Miss Paxton. "You can perhaps take comfort in the fact that it has not been announced in the papers."

Hart shot her a quelling look. "I believe I'll take comfort in the fact that my betrothed is kind and—"

A shout sounded from outside.

"Energetic," he finished before he opened the door and strode out onto the terrace. The combatants were quite involved in their battle and didn't notice him, even when he strode out onto the lawn where they fought.

"If you'll permit me to cut in," he began as he came up behind Emily.

With a gasp, she whirled—and whacked him right in the chest with her stick.

"*Oof!*" The shock came from the blow—and from the sight of her. Her eyes flashed with mirth, her skin glowed with health and exertion. She was laughing and happy and beautiful and . . . . so very alive.

He ignored the snort from Miss Paxton's direction. "Good afternoon, Emily," he said with a short bow.

"My lord," she curtsied and sparkled up at him.

"I admit, this isn't what I expected when I asked that you move quietly through society for the next few weeks."

"Ah, well. We so rarely get what we expect in life, my lord." She laughed. "I daresay it's a good lesson for you." She shot a conspirator's glance at his young cousin. "And James here will not tell tales on me, will you James?"

Ignoring the boy's assurances, Hart waved to the growing audience at the windows. "No, but they might." He knew his own reaction would influence the others, though, and took care to show his good humor. "So if you'll agree to let me take over the lesson, I'll show young James a true *en garde* stance?"

He shot her a grin, bowed low over her hand, took her stick from her and turned to the boy.

***

Emily stared in horror at her audience. Had she committed a social gaffe on her first outing? She held her chin high—and lifted it even higher when she saw that Miss Paxton was in the group at the terrace windows—and she was grinning in gleeful malice.

Keeping a smile firmly on her face, Emily headed back for the house. She'd tried to help a dejected boy—and might even have succeeded. She hadn't done anything wrong—and even if she had, she would never admit it in front of that spiteful cat.

"Well, I'm glad to see your gown has taken no damage," the countess said thoughtfully as she came in.

"The modistes in America must be very busy, if this is how the young ladies conduct their social calls." Miss Paxton did not even wait for an introduction to begin her cutting remarks. Emily shot her a haughty glance even as she waited, breathless on the inside, to see if the girl would recognize her.

But like everyone else, Miss Paxton saw what she expected. And what she saw was a rival, if her look of disdain was any indication.

But the marchioness was still staring outside at her son as he faced off against Hart and laughed at something the earl said. She made a strange sound and turned to face them, her hands clasped in front of her and her face oddly red.

"Oh, you *darling* girl," she said on a whisper, and she clasped Emily and pulled her to her bosom. She pushed her away, staring into her face and pulled her close again. "You cannot know how worried I've been. Since the accident James has been so distant and dejected.

He won't talk, he barely eats, he won't try anything for fear of failure. I vow he hasn't smiled since it happened—and look at him now!" She held Emily by the shoulders. "How did you *do* it?"

"I'm afraid I spoke very disparagingly to him," Emily admitted. "It did the trick, as it often does with boys."

"Bless you, a thousand times!"

The marchioness kissed her—and her fate was sealed.

Lady Feltham spread the tale far and wide, lauding Emily as a worker of miracles and everyone who had been curious before was on fire to meet her now. They all wished to know the American who had captured Hartford and brought Feltham's young heir back to life.

She met scores of people. She and the countess were invited everywhere. She went on calls and to dinners, on walks in the parks and on outings to see the sites. Miss Mary Carmichael became a friend and companion and Emily won over all the smaller Carmichaels by sewing them tiny costumes for the figures in their toy theatre. Her social engagements were reported in the papers, as was her wardrobe. Madame Lalbert's business doubled.

Not everything was sunny, though. There were whispered resentments that Hart had chosen his bride from outside of the *ton*. The girls who started that one were jealous, she felt sure—and she felt sure that Miss Paxton had had a hand in it too. They were convinced that she was not good enough for Hart. They were right, of course, but she'd be damned before she gave them the satisfaction of knowing it.

She still saw very little of him—and that gave rise to rumors that she was his mother's pick and that Hart was reluctant to seal the deal.

Once or twice she did spot the Duke of Danby at a social event, but he didn't seem to notice her. Only at Lady Atherton's musicale did she feel that he looked at her for longer than was strictly necessary, but he faded into the crowd and she didn't see him again, although she suffered through some very questionable musical offerings while she watched for him.

The very worst news came when Hart arrived to take her for a drive. It started out well. She wore white poplin skirts trimmed in blue, with her blue pelisse—a happy coincidence, since Hart arrived decked in buff and blue. They looked like they belonged together—and the thought sent a flush rising into her cheeks.

Had she ever noticed how wide his shoulders were? Or how large and competent his hands? He took hers to help her up into his phaeton, and she basked in the lovely heat that rose up her arm and stole into the rest of her. She shivered at the feel of it, at once strange and warmly familiar.

"How have you been faring?" she asked, anxious to know that she'd done the job he'd hired her for. "How is your work going? Are you accomplishing all that you wished?"

"Much of it," he answered as they set off for Hyde Park and the fashionable strut.

"Have you caught up on the new agricultural developments that will make your estates more profitable?"

"Some. A couple of committees are hammering out tariff changes that might be advantageous. And there's a gentleman in Sussex trying to develop a mechanized grain harvester, but it looks to be a ways from being really helpful," he sighed. "But I will not bore you with such talk."

"I'm not bored at all. Never turn down a chance to learn, that's what my Papa told me. You never know when it might become useful."

"I doubt grain harvesters will ever be of use to you," he said with a smile.

"Not so," she insisted. "Papa was a linen draper—and keeping up with the agricultural news was just one of the things that helped him grow his business into a sizable import firm."

"Really?" She'd caught his attention.

"It's true. If the sheep in Norwich suffered from dysentery or foot rot, he'd buy worsted before the price could go up. Major storms along the coast of Africa? He'd buy silk." She shrugged. "He'd turn a tidy profit when others could not afford to renew their stock."

"Interesting."

"All the world is interesting, Hart." She flung a hand out to indicate the busy street and the people upon it. "'It's a grand, big world,' he used to tell me. 'But small too, once you open your eyes to see the connections between us.'"

"Your father sounds like a smart man."

"He was," she said softly.

"Something tells me you take after him."

The approval in his tone sent a different sort of yearning through her. She tried to tamp it down. Her heart ached a little more each time she saw him, she had to start guarding it before she did something foolish.

"I'd be honored to have it thought so. He was a wonderful father and husband."

"You and your mother must miss him very much."

He was fishing, and she knew it—but she allowed it. "We do," she said. "Now, tell me, have we accomplished what you wanted? I know I've not exactly been quiet, but I have drawn the *ton's* attention. Has it worked for you—are you left alone?"

"The gentlemen have been curious, but are easily put off by a word or two."

"And the young ladies?" She held her breath.

"They've turned their attention elsewhere," he assured her, "but for one persistent young miss."

"Who is it?" she asked, mentally sifting through the girls she'd met.

"Miss Paxton," he answered with a tinge of distaste.

"Miss Paxton?" Her own aversion rang loud. "But she is already betrothed!"

"So I gathered, yet she keeps showing up like a bad penny." He maneuvered his team through the gates to the park.

"I'd heard that the Earl of Ardman had gone to his estates."

"Well, I wish he would come back and take the girl in hand," Hart grumbled. "I'm at Grillon's and I swear, she dines there more than I do. She's growing bold too, hinting that a betrothal is but a promise that may yet be broken."

Anger and protectiveness surged in her breast. That sneaky cat. She would not sink her claws into Hart. "It's one thing for her to disparage me," she said, furious. "But I will not allow her to pester you."

"Disparage you?" he asked.

Emily rolled her eyes. "She is behind fully half of the rumors that circulate about me—definitely the ones that say I am too coarse to be your Countess."

Now Hart was riled. "That is ridiculous," he began.

But they had turned onto Rotten Row and the crowds descended. The phaeton was besieged with friends of his and acquaintances of hers, all wishing to exchange a few polite words. They barely moved for nearly thirty minutes, and through it all, Emily's brain was churning. The sparkle of the Serpentine caught her eye through the trees—and inspiration struck.

"Hart," she said suddenly. "Would you walk with me along the water?"

"If you wish." He hesitated. "But my tiger will not be able to follow along."

She laughed. "That, my lord, is the idea."

He assisted her to the ground and they strolled off, leaving the throng behind. Very deliberately she leaned into him as they walked. Determination coursed through her. Moving casually, she turned to smile at him, but aimed herself so that she could see behind.

Yes. As expected, a few people had followed their example. And Miss Paxton, dragging her maid along by the elbow, was one of them.

Perfect.

And it would be perfect, were their circumstances different. He felt so warm and solid beside her. Safe was not a feeling she'd experienced much since her papa died, but walking next to him, she felt . . . protected. As if nothing could go wrong.

Except everything could go very wrong, if she did not take care. And if she did not keep Miss Paxton from becoming an even greater pest.

She sighed.

"You know, there was one other reason I wanted some freedom this Season," he said, "in addition to the ones we've already discussed."

"Oh?" She glanced back again to make sure their followers were still coming.

"Yes. I'd hoped to have a chance to look around at the young women at my leisure. You know, without worrying that a dance would be willfully mistaken for a proposal."

She swallowed. "And have you? Looked around at the young women? And found one you might not mind pursuing further than a dance?"

"I believe I may have," he said softly.

She tossed her head. "But you don't *know*?" It came out a bit scornfully.

"I don't *know*," he agreed easily. "But I find I don't know anything like I thought I did. For instance, I know the birds are singing. I know the breeze is rustling the leaves in the trees, but all I feel is your arm in mine and all I hear is the beat of my heart and the slide of silk over your skin."

She stopped and looked up at him.

And there it was. Potential. Pull. Energy and almost a living temptation dancing between them—openly acknowledged at last.

How she wished this was a real fork in the road. A place where she could choose to chase potential, chase him. But she hadn't been born the lady he needed, and she wouldn't allow herself to fill any other role in his life.

So she breathed deeply, experienced fully the beauty of this moment—and then pulled it to a halt.

"Very pretty, Hart, but save it for when we have an audience."

His expression stilled. She took the opportunity to steer him toward several stands of trees off to the left. He went along, but looked down at her with a very real question in his eyes. "What is it that we are doing, Emily?"

She straightened her spine. "I'm showing Miss Paxton that I keep my promises."

She pulled him behind a tree and he went willingly. She positioned him so that his back was against a hickory and she was facing back the way they'd come. She edged an eye out, saw Miss Paxton hurrying in their direction, and ducked back.

"What are you doing now?" Hart asked. He hadn't let her avoidance upset him. In fact, he now looked amused.

"I'm judging the best timing of the thing."

"This is a new side of you, Emily. Very martial."

"Yes, well, I'm the general in the campaign for your freedom, am I not?" She clutched his arms. "Wait. Wait. A moment longer. Now!"

Stepping close, she pulled him down and kissed him.

Hart stiffened. Then he put his hand on her waist and she jumped at the jolt that darted through her at the contact.

"You started it," he murmured.

And then his lips touched hers again. And she was gone. Lost in a sweet, sharp ache that only grew as his arms slipped around her to gather her close. His mouth teased her, tempted her, coaxed with a questing tongue and she answered, melting against him as he seared her, claimed her with the heat of his kiss.

Good heavens. They were molded together, her breasts pressing against his coat, his hands moving over her, across the small of her back, and over the curve of her hips. Fire flared between them. Her hands crept upward, clutched those broad shoulders close for one more long, delicious moment—then she pushed away.

She stared into his dark eyes for the space of one heartbeat, two, then glanced over towards the water. Miss Paxton and her maid had moved away and joined the group of others at the shore.

"There," she said in a shaky voice. "We showed her, didn't we?"

Chapter Six

Hart was in trouble. He'd hired Emily so that he could take his mind off of marriage-minded misses and concentrate on his work. Instead, as each day passed, he grew more and more focused on his faux fiancé—and it had only grown worse since that kiss in the park.

He'd never met a woman like her. She was down to earth, kind, practical, a curvy goddess. Yet at the same time she was quick and witty and somehow fit seamlessly into her role as a Young Society Miss. And she felt protective toward him. Toward *him*. The novelty of it amused him almost as much as the sweetness of it touched him.

Strangely, since all he'd wanted was to avoid the girls who longed to become mistress of Hartsworth, he kept thinking that he'd like to show it to Emily.

He felt sure that she would love the Great Hall, with the galleries and the fireplace big enough to roast an ox. He could clearly see her rejoicing in the summer roses in the enclosed garden. Her practical side would be as aghast as his at the price of those custom windows, surely. But would she believe in the family ghosts? And would his great-great-grandmother visit her, as she did every time a new heir to Hartsworth was conceived?

Oh, Lord. He was in so much trouble.

Since he was currently unable to focus on the never-ending debate over the Corn Laws, he took himself off to White's. He still needed to track down Peter Grant.

He found his friend this time, poring over the papers in the Morning Room. Hart took a seat next to him, called a porter to bring a bottle of brandy, and poured two drinks.

"A drink is the least I owe you, since I missed that lecture we planned to attend—and since I'd like to hear what you took away from it," he said with a grin.

"I should thank you for turning me onto it," Peter said, raising his glass. "I'll put what I learned to use at my mother's estate in Yorkshire."

They talked of grain strains and planting techniques for the better part of the bottle, before Peter claimed prior plans and left him. Hart drank on, and when a pack of Town bucks came by, offering a night of drinking and gaming, he threw his hands up and went along.

He had sense enough to know that he'd already done too much of the former to be any good at the latter, so he continued the evening as he'd started, contenting himself with watered-down whisky and a role as cheerleader at the E.O. wheel.

Even watered whisky has an effect, though, especially after half a bottle of brandy, and it was still early when he realized that he was properly soused—as far below the mahogany as he'd been since his school days.

Intent on heading home, he got to his feet, only to stumble before he'd gone a couple of steps.

One of his friends caught him. "Whoa! Easy now, Hartford. Where are you heading?"

"Home," he mumbled. "Need to sleep it off."

"Hold on a moment. You're in no shape to get there on your own. Ho, Hamilton!" the young man summoned another one of the group. "We can stop off at Portman Square on the way to the hell, can we not?"

Hamilton tossed a sour look over Hart. "Aye. If he's not going to gamble, then we might as well drop him off before he starts to puke. Come on lads," he called. "We're off!"

The crowded hackney ride was naught but a blur. Hart only knew it was over when he found himself standing on the pavement before his house, listening to the whoops and hollers of the others fade as the hack moved on.

He stumbled to the door and stood frowning at it. Why did it not open?

"Wait." Only then did he realize his friends had dropped him at Herrington House. "I'm not staying here."

He turned to catch them, but the coach had already rounded the corner.

He turned back and blinked stupidly at the door—and thought longingly of his bed upstairs, so much closer than Grillon's.

He shouldn't. Even in his cups he knew it was a bad idea. But the world was spinning and if it didn't stop he was going to cast up his accounts on the stoop. Spreading his arms, he leaned against the door to steady it—or himself. Either would do.

He misjudged the distance, though, and thunked his temple on the wood.

"Ow." It was all he got out before the world shifted—or the door opened. Same difference. He stumbled into his entry hall and onto his knees. The trip was more than his addled brain could take, and he groaned and sunk the rest of the way down.

"My lord?" It was Williams. "Are you all right?"

Instead of answering, Hart rolled over and blinked up at him.

"We weren't expecting you," the footman fretted. "The ladies decided on an evening in tonight and everyone is abed."

"Don't wake them." Oh, Lord, had he shouted that? "Wrong house. Don't worry. I'm leaving."

Williams pushed and pulled and managed to get him upright. "Perhaps you'd better rest here tonight, sir." He struggled to catch his breath and prop Hart up at the same time.

"Yes! Just a rest." He hoped that came out in a whisper. "Just a moment to stop the spin and then I'll move on."

"Shall I help you upstairs, sir?"

Hart snorted. "No, for then I'll have to navigate my way back down and no one wants that."

"No, sir." Williams shook his head vigorously.

"I'm not staying. Just get me to a chair for a few moments."

He leaned heavily on the man and in moments the parlor sofa loomed comfortingly ahead. "Ah. Just the thing. Good man." He stretched out and closed his eyes.

"Just for a moment . . ." he murmured.

* * *

How decadent she had become. Past midnight and she could not sleep because she'd become used to late nights.

Her stomach growled. And late suppers.

She hadn't wished to stay in tonight. She hadn't wanted to have any quiet time in which to reflect on that kiss. But the countess had pleaded a headache and here she was, with plenty of time to think of Hart's sweet words, the electric shock of his hands at her back and the wicked temptation of his mouth on hers. She thought of the incredible breadth of his shoulders and the unyielding strength of his body pressed against her. She imagined it happening again. Imagined a lifetime of such kisses—and she wanted to cry.

But she would not.

She was having a magical, once-in-a-lifetime-Season. She was helping a worthy man. She was being paid handsomely for it, which would enable her to make her mother's life comfortable once more.

She *refused* to cry.

Her stomach rumbled again and she decided to eat something instead. Cook had made a huge batch of that delicious baked rice with truffles. Surely there was some left in the kitchens?

No need to wake anyone. She went down the back stairs, rummaged around and helped herself. Once she was pleasantly full, but still not sleepy, she decided to wander to the study in search of a novel.

She was reaching for the knob on the study door when a sudden, snorting snore came out of the darkness. It repeated, then settled into a steady rhythm.

She froze.

A servant, asleep at his station? Most likely. Still, she whirled, intending to retreat to her room, and ran straight into an occasional table with her shin. She swore under her breath and dropped her candle.

And with another snort, the snoring abruptly stopped.

* * *

Something woke him.

A thunk? A crash? A gasp?

He hardly knew—but he was happy to wake to clarity. The alcoholic fog had lifted. He felt remarkably alert—as if his life had suddenly snapped into focus.

And his focus was on Emily. On her loyalty, her sweet, protective nature. On how she saw people so clearly. On how her generous mouth felt under his and those voluptuous curves felt pressed to his chest.

It wasn't enough. He wanted more. All of her, to be his now and forever. It was utterly apparent—they were meant to be together.

If only he hadn't painstakingly created the situation that made it impossible.

Another thunk and a whispered curse had him turning his head. A faint glow shone from the hall.

It would be her. Down here. With him. Of course it would.

The universe and the heavens and fate—they were all trying to tell him something. He would listen—especially as it was so ardently what he wanted to hear.

She was fiddling with her candle outside the study. "Oh, it's you." It wasn't relief in her tone.

Good.

"I meant to fetch a candle . . . I mean, a book. A novel to help me sleep."

Her hair was down. Just like in his fantasies. She had it loosely gathered into a thick, ebony braid that snaked over her shoulder and pointed the way down to her glorious bosom. "Which one?" he asked.

"I . . . uh . . ." The candle finally straight, she glanced up at him. She seemed nervous.

Good.

"Which book? If you could have your choice?" he clarified.

"Oh. Ah, *Ivanhoe*, I guess."

"A good choice."

"Young James reminded me of how much I enjoyed *Lady of the Lake* . . ." her words trailed away and her chin lifted. "I had to sell my books when my father's business failed." She bit the words out. "The strain of it killed him and my mother and I have had no money for such things since. The few books I've read in the last years have only come by the kindness of Mr. Finch, a fence who gives me first crack at the volumes pawned in his shop."

She was trying to emphasize the differences between them. Hart shook his head. He only admired her more. "I don't have a copy of *Ivanhoe* in Town. Only stodgy history and agriculture here. All of my novels are in the library at home."

"Oh." She turned away. "Goodnight, then."

He grasped her arm to keep her from going. Pulling her back, he took the candle from her, set it on the table and pressed a kiss to her forehead. Her head tipped back—and there was no resisting her. He let his fingers drift up to caress her jaw, then he brushed her mouth with his, and lingered.

With a small sound of surrender, she kissed him back. His hands drifted, caressing her neck and shoulders before traveling down the curve of her back and pulling her closer.

The kiss deepened. Desire built steadily, stirring up a flaring sense of want. Need.

Her hands slipped under his coat, burrowed further beneath his waistcoat. The feather-soft touch, so brave and shy at once, made him wild.

He buried his face in her neck and breathed her in.

"Hartsworth is an estate," he said thickly.

"What?" Her back had arched and she made a lovely offering, just waiting for the guidance of his touch—and his lips and his teeth.

No. Not yet. But she would be his.

He lifted his head and gazed into her eyes. "It's my estate. Not a jeweled crown. A castle, really—given to one of my ancestors—a knight who defeated a dastardly villain and won a beautiful bride."

"Oh." She sounded dazed. And like she didn't much care.

"Every age has seen a famous love story at Hartsworth. Before this is over, I'm going to take you there," he vowed. "I'll tell you all the stories. I'll show you everything. All the things that I love. All the eccentricities and the extravagances that drive me mad. I think you'll love it as much as I do."

He kissed her again—hard, demanding and quick. Then he smiled down into her wondering face, brushed her cheek, whirled on his heel and left.

Chapter Seven

He was not living in her pocket, still, but Hart had begun to show her a good deal of consideration. He sent her a huge bouquet of glorious pink roses and a note saying no other flower could do justice to her hair and eyes. He took her driving twice more. He still did not partake of many of the Season's entertainments, but he visited her box at the theatre during intermission and he showed up to walk through the Egyptian Gallery of the British Museum during her visit there with the Carmichaels.

"Is Hartsworth really so lovely an estate?" she asked the Countess at breakfast one morning. "I can't see that it could be so impressive as to make the young ladies act so foolishly—not when Hart himself is about."

"Ah, someone told you about Hartsworth, then?" Lady Hartford said, watching her over the rim of her cup.

"Hart told me that it is an estate, and it made me remember some whispers that I'd heard— but I thought they were talking about some sort of tiara."

"Hart told you?" his mother repeated. Why did she sound incredulous?

"Yes." Hart had told her—and clearly it meant something to them, although she couldn't figure it out. He was being everything kind and solicitous and Emily began to wonder if he was trying to convince the *ton* of his regard—or her.

It was useless to know which she hoped it would turn out to be.

She doubted he would turn up at tonight's entertainment. It was a literary salon hosted by Lord and Lady Ellesworth. She hadn't thought anything of the invitation when it came, save for being pleased to be one of the ladies asked to read, but she'd paused at her first glimpse of the baroness.

She knew her. Miss Glenna Bolton, she had once been. They shared blood.

Lady Ellesworth was the *legitimate* granddaughter of the Duke of Danby's sister Georgina. Emily was her illegitimate counterpart.

A baroness now, Glenna had once been a shopkeeper, just like Emily's parents. She'd kept a bookshop. Emily had stopped in once, giving in to curiosity. Glenna had run the shop and looked after her grandfather, who had slept in a chaise by the window during her visit.

Emily relaxed now, remembering. The girl had not known her then, of a certainty she would not, now.

She couldn't help but be tense, though, when Lady Ellesworth approached to thank her for taking part in the readings, but the baroness was everything welcoming.

"How did you make your selection for tonight, Miss Latham? I was surprised by your choice. An American devotee of Mr. Burns?"

"I am indeed a devotee, my lady. He speaks to something inside of me." She paused. "Thank you for the loan of your copy of his works. I'm glad there is someone else here tonight who enjoys him."

"Oh, I do. I was wondering, however, if you have traveled to Scotland?"

"I hope to, very soon," she hedged.

"You will love it, I feel sure. In the meantime, are you enjoying your stay in London?"

"I am. London is a wonderful city—full of so many layers." She wasn't strictly lying, but still, she hated the subterfuge. The baroness did not deserve it.

"It is, at that." The other woman cocked her head. "Do you find yourself homesick?"

Emily gave her a crooked smile. "I miss my mother dreadfully."

The baroness nodded. "Family is a wonderful thing, is it not?" She watched Emily closely, as if the question were an important one.

"Family is *everything*," Emily answered that one easily.

"I am glad I am not the only one who thinks so." Lady Ellesworth nodded toward the surrounding crowd. "But friends are important too."

"Some friends become the family that you choose," Emily agreed, thinking of Jasper.

"Indeed—as do husbands." The baroness gave a melting look towards her own, across the room.

Emily flushed and buried a sharp pang of longing. "If one is lucky enough to choose the right husband."

Lady Ellesworth's gaze snapped back. "Did you not choose Lord Hartford?"

She hesitated, unsure what would be best to say. "He was chosen for me," she said at last, "but I accepted him." She sighed and gave a shrug. "And I'm glad I did."

The baroness raised her glass. "Here's to family and friendship." She drank, and then smiled. "I like you, Miss Latham."

Emily tipped her own glass. "Likewise, Lady Ellesworth."

The readings began and soon enough it was her turn. She took her spot on the dais and opened her book of poems by Robert Burns.

"I've chosen one of my favorites, *The Flowering Banks of Cree*," she told the audience. "I hope you will enjoy it."

The room grew quiet as she began and she tried to do the sweet words justice. She had reached the line

At once 'tis music and 'tis love

when she felt the first tingle. All the hairs on her neck and arms stood up in a sudden, sensual awareness. She glanced up to see Hart at the back of the room, his gaze intent on her. She read on, and when she reached the lines welcoming love, she raised her gaze again, to meet his full on.

She took her bow at the end, but the polite applause was dulled by a thick fog. He was here—and the shimmering, dancing energy between them was the only thing that cut through the haze.

He came forward and took her hand as she descended, leading her to the back of the Lady Ellesworth's music room. When she would have taken a seat in the back row, he tugged her onward.

She followed and he led her toward the back of the house to a tiny parlor.

"This is likely for the family's use and not a guest room at all," she objected in a whisper.

"Yes, which means that we'll be left alone here," he returned. "I have a gift for you and I wished to give it in private."

"A gift?" She frowned past a surge of excitement. "That wasn't part of our agreement, my lord."

"I think you'll forgive me. Close your eyes."

She did, her heart pounding. And he set something big, solid and heavy in her hands.

A book. "*Ivanhoe*," she whispered, her eyes filling.

"So you can start your own collection again," he said softly.

A tear leaked out and she closed her eyes against the rest. "Thank you," she whispered.

His thumb traced the tear, then his hand cupped her jaw and he was kissing her. The book impeded them, but she clutched it tight and refused to let go, leaning in and opening her mouth to his as a different path to intimacy.

For that's what they were creating with each sigh and every pleasurable stroke of their tongues. Heavens yes, they desired each other, but this was deeper than a kiss, beyond mere desire. They were spiraling into sensual, heady depths of knowing. Of certainty. Of the promise of everything more.

"Hart," she breathed at last. "This is a mistake."

He leaned his forehead against hers. "Very likely. But still, we are going to make it."

"Are we?" she asked.

"Together."

"How?" She grew near tears again, from frustration and longing. "It's impossible. We've made it so."

"We'll find a way." He said it fiercely. A vow.

She only nodded, letting in a first, small tendril of hope.

"I can't stay. I have a late committee meeting. But I couldn't keep away, not entirely." He kissed her again, quickly, and set her away.

"Thank you for the gift."

"And thank you for yours."

She hadn't given him a gift. But she knew what he meant. And it filled her heart.

He bowed over her hand and left.

And she sat, holding her book and dreaming . . . for who knows how long.

* * *

It was footsteps that roused her. Soft, but steady. Emily arose from the plush chair where she'd been drifting. She didn't want to get caught in here. She didn't really wish to talk to anyone at all, but she supposed she would go and put the book with her wrap and go back to the readings—once whoever was in the passage had passed.

Except the footsteps slowed. Were they coming in here? Feeling slightly panicked and a little silly, she slipped behind the door.

The creak of another door led her to peek through the crack into the passageway. A green baize servant's door, just beyond her room and on the other side, cracked open. A maid slid through—and met up with Miss Paxton.

"Did anyone see you leave?" the young lady demanded.

"No, Miss."

Emily was suddenly and incredibly glad they could not see her.

"Do you still have the vial?"

"Yes, Miss." She didn't sound happy about it.

"Keep it safely tucked away. Lord Hartford has already come and gone. We've missed our chance tonight—but we will catch him at his aunt's ball. He'll be obligated to stay the night through."

The maid ducked her head. "Yes, Miss," she whispered.

"Don't go soft on me now," Miss Paxton snapped. She crossed to the parlor where Emily hid and peeked in. Finding it empty and only dimly lit, she turned and struck the doorframe as she turned back, making Emily jump and her grip on the large book slip. She hung on and pressed back against the wall.

"Damn my father, in any case," Miss Paxton hissed. "We wouldn't have to get up to this scheming if he would only consent to follow Lord Ardman home."

"Will he not relent, Miss? It seems so much . . . safer, to take care of it that way."

"He will not. He doesn't find it *seemly*."

"I know it leaves you in desperate straits, but Lord Hartford does seem happy with his betrothed."

"Damn her, too. Pushy American. Lord Hartford is the right height and coloring—and if I have to trap a man then it might as well be one who owns an estate like Hartsworth." She paused. "That castle might make all of this worry and bother worth it, at that."

Emily sucked in a shocked, silent breath and her fingers, bloodless from gripping the book so tightly, slipped. Ivanhoe's heavy cover fell forward and hit the door, making a small but definite thud.

The other two women froze. Miss Paxton pushed the maid forward and pointed to the parlor door. The poor girl moved past Emily's view, looking in, then came back, shrugging.

"Back to the kitchens with you, then," the young lady commanded. "I'll go back to the party."

Emily sighed in relief as the two went their separate ways, then allowed a great blaze of anger to roar high. She stalked down the passage, her mind a whirl of fury and resolve.

She stopped when she reached the music room again and found Miss Paxton standing in the doorway with a small group, gaze fastened on the passage. When she saw Emily emerge, she speared her with a glare of narrowed eyes.

Emily stopped and returned the disdainful glance, lifting her chin.

The gauntlet had been thrown and accepted. The challenge was on.

Chapter Eight

Emily had once seen an electric machine. The showman had flipped a switch and jagged lines of electricity had shot out in every direction. She currently felt just like that sphere—and each jagged bolt of electricity arcing from her was a different emotion.

She wanted Hart. Finally admitting it, contemplating the real possibility, filled her with hope and despair.

She wanted to *strangle* Miss Paxton. No matter what happened or what it cost her, Emily was determined that that harpy would not get her claws into Hart.

Most of all, she wanted her mother.

Now *that*, she had some control over. She boxed up her ball gown, told the countess that she had an appointment to have it fitted, took Molly for propriety, and set out for Madame Lalbert's.

Miss Carmichael was there, showing off the last fitting for her new ball gown in the outer room. Emily admired it with everyone else, nodded at the other customer choosing fabrics in the corner and asked Madame if she might have Mrs. Spencer's help with her dress.

The front door bell rang again as another customer entered, but Emily didn't pause to see who it was. She moved purposefully toward the back, and when her mother pulled the curtain shut, she tossed the box aside and fell into her arms. "Oh, Mama! It's terrible!"

"Oh, my darling, what is it?" Her mother clutched her tightly. "What's happened? Is it Lord Hartford?"

"No. Yes." Her voice broke. "I don't know!"

Breaking away to hold her face in her hands, her mother scanned her. Her eyes darted about—and then her face fell. "Oh, dear. You've done it, haven't you? Fallen in love with him?"

Emily bit her lip. "How can you tell?"

"Your glow, your flush. The light of joy and the shadow of fear in your eye." Her shoulders slumped. "Oh, my dear, I warned you against this."

"I didn't mean to," Emily whispered.

"No. We never do, do we?" She sank down on a nearby stool. "I didn't want this for you! I don't want you to know the pain of always waiting on someone who will never be there for you."

"It isn't like that, Mama." She knelt at her mother's feet and laid her head in her lap. "He loves me too."

Her mother heaved a sigh. "Well, that is something." She thought a moment as her fingers shifted in Emily's hair. "But, how—I still don't see—"

"I know!" Emily interrupted her in despair. "There's no way forward for us—and that isn't even the worst part. There is a wicked girl . . ." She told her mother everything, then and, looking up, watched her grow whiter as the story went on.

"Good heavens, this is much more complicated than I could have imagined." She stood and pulled Emily to her feet too. "I think perhaps we should put an end to this."

"No! I cannot leave yet. I will not let Miss Paxton hurt him."

"Have you warned him?"

"I sent him an urgent message, but he is in Richmond interviewing a land agent and will not likely see it until tonight. I have to warn him—and I know you are right. I have to finish this. But, oh—I don't want to! That horrid girl has stolen my last days with him." A sob broke through. "Mama, what am I going to do?"

Before her mother could answer, the curtain was swept open. Emily turned in horror to find Miss Paxton standing there in terrible triumph. "Mama!" she repeated. "Your mother?" She stared between the two of them. "I knew it! I knew there was something wrong about you! You're a *fraud*!"

Emily stepped forward to shield her mother. "And what do you think you are?" she asked the girl.

Miss Paxton looked surprised, but then she gave them an ugly grin. "I think I am the winner, you tart!"

"Katharine! Do hurry!" It was Mrs. Paxton calling. "I told you we did not have time to stop in."

"I'm coming, Mother," she answered, never taking her gaze off of Emily. She moved forward and grabbed Emily's wrist. "I have you now," she said, low and harsh. "Don't think you can wiggle out of it. You will meet me tomorrow at Lady Feltham's ball and I will have instructions for you. Do not think to warn Lord Hartford. I *will* know. I have eyes on you, Miss Latham . . . or whatever your real name is. How do you think I knew where to find you just now? If I see any attempt to contact the earl, I will go straight to the papers with this story and ruin you all. Do you understand me?"

Emily's mother stepped forward and pulled her away. "Take your hands off of my daughter."

"Katharine!"

"Coming!"

She sneered at them. "You will leave now, as well, so that I know you are not conspiring." Holding the curtain aside, she said, "Let us go."

Emily glared at her, then turned and gave her mother a hug. "Send Jasper," she whispered. Then, with a nod, she followed the evil girl out.

* * *

The hour had grown late when Hart returned from Richmond. His tread slowed as he climbed the stairs to his rooms, but he felt good about the man he'd hired to oversee his property in Shropshire. The land had been his own, inherited from an uncle long before John had died and the earldom had been thrust upon him. He'd relocated some of his experiments to

Hartsworth and hoped to recreate some of the customizations he'd made on his green houses, but a few of his projects were tied to the land and he hoped he'd found someone to carry them on and keep him—

"Excuse me, sir."

A boy sat on the threshold of his apartment.

"I come from Miss Spencer—and no one is supposed to know."

Hart fished out his key. "Then come in and quickly." He ushered the boy in. "Did anyone see you?"

"No." The boy yawned. "I been waiting in the servant's stair a while, but then I started to fall asleep and I was afraid I'd miss you."

"Good man—you haven't missed me." Hart grinned. "Now, what is it that Miss Spencer needs?"

"Read this." He thrust over a piece of parchment, folded small, and Hart snatched it up. A cold mass of anger and worry formed in his stomach as he read it over.

"It's all true," the boy offered up. "Especially the part about them that's watching her. I seen 'em myself. I pretended to deliver gloves to the lady countess and a pair of roughs stopped and searched me on the way in."

"You are Jasper, I presume?" He lifted the note. "She mentions you."

"Aye. They tried to peach me on the way out too, but Em gave me a scone to munch on and I folded it small and stuck it inside. They didn't think nothin' of me holding on to it."

"That explains the stickiness—and the scent of lemon." Hart sat a moment, thinking. Their situation had been difficult before. Now it was perilous indeed. He stilled, remembering Emily's words when they had first made their bargain. She'd been sweet and unworldly enough to think to protect him—but he would be damned before he allowed someone like Miss Paxton to harm the girl he loved.

And love her, he did. How could he not? Look at how she responded to this threat—any of those girls who had thrown themselves at him would have collapsed in terror and tears. Not his Emily. She was thwarting the enemy. He'd wager she was planning on sacrificing herself to save him, too.

He shook his head. He would make sure it wasn't necessary.

"Jasper," he said thoughtfully, "you've been in and out of Herrington House?"

"Aye."

"Do you know the maid, Molly?"

"I could pick her out," the boy answered.

"Good. I want you to go and pick her out— and deliver a message. We'll need her help tonight. And tell her not to tell Emily what we are up to, just in case . . ."

Chapter Nine

She looked magnificent, even if it was vain to think so herself. Madame Lalbert and her mother had outdone themselves. Her dress was white, with a tight, scoop-necked bodice and short, sheer sleeves. It was the embroidery that made it stunning, however. Intricate designs in the deepest, darkest red drew the eye to the neckline and echoed along the flowing skirts. She carried a thick shawl of the same blood-red and her elaborately curled hair featured a silk ribbon in the same hue.

She stared at herself in the mirror and recognized how the striking combination flattered her pale skin and dark hair, and how the cut of the dress emphasized all the best features of her figure. And still, she couldn't help but wish for her old armor.

Oh, how she craved her old invisibility.

But it was not to be. Tonight would likely end in notoriety for her—but only for her, if she could possibly manage it.

Everything depended on her ability to bluff Miss Paxton.

"Hart has sent word that he will meet us at my sister's." The countess was moving through the passageway when Emily emerged. She stopped. "Oh, my dear, you are stunning."

"Thank you," she whispered.

Hart's mother looked her over. "Your first ball, is it not? Nerves are expected," she soothed.

Emily was sick with fury, anxiety, and impending loss, but she couldn't say that. She nodded, instead.

"My dear." The countess gave her hand a kind squeeze. "Will you allow me the chance to thank you? I was unsure about this scheme of Hart's at the beginning—but you have done him good. He appears relaxed . . . even happy . . . for the first time since we lost his brother."

Emily breathed deeply. At least she'd accomplished that. She nodded again. "I'm so glad."

The countess let her go and began to pull on her gloves. "Good. Now, let us go forth and conquer."

She almost laughed. Oh, how she fervently hoped it would be so.

* * *

Young James was in the receiving line and he gallantly requested the first dance with her. Emily was touched and happy to give it. They'd arrived late enough that she didn't have to wait long before they took their places. The young man looked as nervous as she felt, but he successfully navigated the steps and appeared as proud as punch when it ended. And again, Emily felt nearly as proud—here was another good thing she had accomplished. If only her time here was not so quickly ending.

But the end did arrive moments later, with a grimly smiling Miss Paxton. "Won't you take a turn with me, Miss Latham?"

She dragged Emily into an alcove. "Marc— I mean, my men say you've done well so far, following instructions," she began. "I'm glad to know that you are taking this seriously. Just do as I say now and you will emerge from this unscathed and free."

"While you trick Hart into marrying you?" Emily returned with scorn. "I don't think I will make it so easy for you."

Miss Paxton flushed with fast-rising anger. "It's not as if you have much choice."

"I do have a choice." She raised her brow. "Do you even pay attention to the world you live in? Expose us if you will," she challenged. "Hartford is a *man*. Yes, his actions will be frowned upon. Some members of the ton will be scandalized. Others will rather admire him. Either way, it will be a three-week-wonder. Something else will come along to capture Society's attention and because he is a man, Hartford's reputation will recover. By next Season—maybe even by the end of this one— those shocked girls will be vying for his attention again.

The girl looked livid at being challenged. "*Your* reputation won't survive."

Emily laughed. "I don't care. I never meant to stay amongst these people to begin with."

Miss Paxton snarled. "Perhaps you won't be so blasé about your family's welfare. I will have you and your mother arrested."

"For what? Making a fool of you?"

"For presenting yourself with a false name!"

"My mother has nothing to do with any of this. And unless Miss Emmaline Latham decides to leave her new husband and sail across the Atlantic to press charges, I'm afraid the courts will merely laugh at you. Until the earl and his mother testify for me, that is." She gave the girl a look of pity. "You've played your hand and lost. Now do leave us alone."

Emily made to leave, but Miss Paxton reached out and grabbed her. Her color was turning truly alarmingly red as she grew even more furious. "Not so fast," she snarled. "You've forgotten your friend, the modiste. I'll see her ruined, and her shop taken from her."

Now that was a threat that could more easily be accomplished. A few rumors or insinuations and London's gossip-susceptible ladies would decide not to frequent Madame Lalbert at all.

"And you've forgotten the fact that no one in Society has yet figured out your family's dangerous financial situation."

Miss Paxton released her. "You don't know what you are talking about."

"I know what the milliners and the glovers and the coal men and all of the rest of the tradesmen are talking about—the mountain of your family's unpaid bills."

"Tradesmen's gossip? No one would bat an eye. You could say the same about any Society family." She laughed. "So, we are at an impasse. But still, I will win, while you and Hartford and your seamstress friend go up in flames. Come," she gestured. "Shall we go and start a scandal?"

Emily hesitated, but she saw the ugly resolution in the girl's eyes. "Any Society family, you think?" she asked slowly. "How many of those debutantes out there are wearing paste jewels? Only you, I'd wager. But we could ask and take a count."

That shook the evil chit. She turned. "How could you—?" Her eyes narrowed and Emily could nearly see the wheels spinning in her brain. "It was you," she said wonderingly. "How did I miss it? You are that upstart, dirty, little *thief*!"

"Go on and tell that one, too," Emily invited. "And I'll tell them all about Marcus Lionel Holt—and his babe that you carry." She shook her head. "No, I am afraid you will have to settle for taking the father of your child to wed, and leave Hart alone."

Miss Paxton had begun to look wild. "Marcus has no *money*!" she hissed.

"And yet," Emily shrugged.

"No. I will not be beaten by the likes of you! Listen to me! You will go and have a footman tell Lord Hartford to meet you in the garden. There is a bank of flowering Hawthorne beyond the fountain. He will meet you—me— there."

"No."

Abruptly, all of the girl's florid color faded away. And suddenly, the grim look of despair and determination on her face frightened Emily more than all of her angry bluster.

"This is all your fault," Miss Paxton whispered. "All of it. You've left me no choice." She sucked in a long breath. "Now I will remind you of how similar in looks and coloring Marcus and Hartford are. And I will tell you that if you do not do as I say, I will march out to the middle of that dance floor and tell my tale of woe to everyone here. How Hartford found me alone in the park and seduced—No! He brutally forced himself upon me. How I fought, but he laughed and overpowered me and left me without a glance." Her lip curled. "Let his reputation recover from that! Either way, by the slight embarrassment of being caught in a tryst, or by being labeled a depraved abuser—he will pledge himself to marry me tonight."

Aghast, Emily backed away. "You would tell such vile lies about an innocent man—and then force him to claim your child?"

"Without a second's hesitation."

The world tilted and Emily watched her slim chance at happiness sliding away from her. A ringing started up in her ears, but she ignored it. She had to think. She would not lose everything in vain.

"No."

Resolute, she brushed past the wicked girl.

"What are you doing?"

"You are right. It is all my fault. And so I shall tell them all. The whole sordid story, beginning at the night I blackmailed you for a paste earring. I accept the blame for everything." She glared at the girl. "And I will also take a page from your book, Miss Paxton and exercise my imagination. I will tell the same sort of ugly lies about you that you mean to visit upon Hart. Except mine will have a foot in the truth. How you got yourself an entire wardrobe when you cheated a dozen modistes by disparaging their finished work, claiming it was unsatisfactory, and then wearing it anyway. How you cuckolded Lord Ardman. Mr. Holt is here tonight, is he not? His reaction will only help sell the story. I'll tell how you got yourself with child and when Lord Ardman's absence made it impossible to trick him, you masterminded a plot with me to trap Hart into paying the price. It will come down to my word versus yours—and you are the one carrying a fatherless child. I'm sure I can come up with a few more sordid details as I go, too. I shall see how the muse moves me."

"You wouldn't *dare*!"

Emily laughed. "Oh, I would dare. I may be ruined, but I am taking you down with me."

"No!"

"Yes." On wooden feet she left the girl behind and headed for the ballroom.

* * *

Hart moved quickly through his aunt's house, looking for Emily. He knew she was here somewhere and he feared Miss Paxton had cornered her in some out of the way spot and was making her miserable. He searched everywhere, then headed back to the ball room.

From the top of the short stairs he could see almost everything. A country-dance set had started to form—and there. Emily moved down the center, between the two lines.

"Excuse me!" He pushed his way down the stairs, past the stream of guests flowing in and out. "Excuse me!"

He lost her when he reached the bottom, but threaded through the crowd toward the dance floor.

"Excuse me!" It was her voice this time, echoing his words. He heard her as he drew closer, but couldn't see her yet. "I'm very sorry to interrupt the pleasantries," she said loudly. "But I'm afraid I have something to confess!"

Hart abandoned politeness and began to shoulder his way through. He could judge his progress by gasps and protests and exclamations.

Not fast enough.

"I'm afraid I must offer my apologies to you all!" She was still talking over people. "I'm afraid I've lied to you. You see, my name is not Emmaline Latham."

Quiet settled around her and Hart broke through the crowd. Too late.

Confused murmurs and questions spread around them. He moved toward her, holding up a hand. "There is no need, my love."

Tears welled, making her grey eyes shine. "There is, I'm afraid. You don't know, Hart, the evil intent she carries."

"It doesn't matter," he began.

"It does. The things she means to say . . ." She shook her head.

"It's all over already, my darling. Her maid knows all of the truth. Molly convinced her to throw her lot in with us. I've spoken with the girl. She's safely ensconced at Herrington House."

A small, strangled sound made him look up into the ring around them, where Miss Paxton's wide eyes conveyed her panic. He took pleasure in continuing. "She's already told her story to the lady's father. And to the magistrate."

The young lady sobbed, then whirled and fled. Hart ignored her and turned to Emily, who, though still paler than he'd seen her, showed signs of fledgling hope.

"Truly?" she whispered.

The crowd muttered in confusion.

She looked around. "It's too late, Hart. I have to tell them who I am. I will deal with the consequences, and then, maybe—"

"What is all of this?" someone demanded.

"I don't know who the chit was supposed to be in the first place," someone else complained.

"What's kind of theatrics are these?" a woman asked.

"Tell us what you mean to say!"

Hart turned to address them, but stilled as the elderly Duke of Danby stepped forward to enter the open circle around them.

"Perhaps my great niece will allow me to explain."

Chapter Ten

Emily's mouth fell open. She had to fight the instinctive urge to duck and run and yet she also suffered the strange compulsion to throw her arms around the older man.

But the duke was not waiting for her wayward emotions to catch up. He strolled around the small space, nodding at acquaintances and generally showing off. "You are privileged to be here for the telling of a good story—one that you will dine off of for months to come," he said affably. He pointed to Hart. "And it starts last Season."

Emily exchanged glances with Hart, but he merely shrugged and waved for the old man to continue.

"Now, you all know how I feel about the matrimonial state." He paused for the titter that ran through the crowd. "I am generally a fan of those maneuvers that see a well matched couple safely wed. But the shenanigans that some of our own young ladies got up to last Spring . . . they went beyond the pale. Shameless." He shook his head. "And unfair, to a family—and to a young man—still mourning a sad loss."

More than one debutante turned her eyes to the ground.

"The same sort of trouble started up again at the beginning of this Season. Didn't it?" He looked around. "But one young woman went so far as to resort to trickery, subterfuge and blackmail."

"And lies," Emily interjected.

"Just so." The duke nodded. "Lord Hartford, being a smart man, called for help." He walked over and took her hand. "My great niece, Miss Emily Spencer, answered."

She gripped him hard. She was filled with gratitude. The duke was telling only the truth, even if he was adjusting the timeline. She should object, she supposed, but if it saved Hart from censure, if it gave them a chance—then she would not quibble.

"Some of you may not be happy that she did it under an assumed name, but let me assure you that she did so with Hestia Wright's guidance and my full knowledge, as well as that of Hartford and his esteemed mother, the countess."

She blinked at him. Was it true? Was he why Hestia Wright had developed a sudden interest in her? She might have been indignant about it yesterday, but now she felt more than ready to forgive. After all, his manipulations had led her to Hart.

Talk started up again and some of it sounded angry to her ears—but she didn't care. The duke was giving them a gift that she would not scorn. And she couldn't keep from staring at Hart—or prevent all that she was feeling from showing.

"Some of you may be persuaded to hold her birth against her."

There were several murmurs of disgusted assent.

"But I confess, I would find this a disappointment—especially considering the fact that we have more than one of the royal natural children amongst us this evening." He paused to let that sink in, and then raised Emily's hand higher. "This girl is my blood. My family. She is the granddaughter of my beloved sister Georgina and she will always be welcome in my homes."

Emily, through tears, thought that the plural use of that last word—and its reminder of the duke's wealth and power—might help drive his point home.

"She will always be welcome at Elleshaven as well." Lady Ellesworth stepped out into the open circle and took her other hand. "I am thrilled to find that you are my cousin."

Emily bit her lip.

"I'll bandy sticks with you any day," young James said valiantly, stepping forward.

"Yes, she is as family here," echoed Lady Feltham.

"She will always be family," the countess said.

"She is always welcome in our home, as well." Mrs. Carmichael stumbled forward after a little push from a teary-eyed Mary.

"And mine," someone called. The swell of support and dissent began to rumble across the room. Hart silenced it when he stepped forward and raised his hands. She waited to hear what he had to say, along with the rest of them.

"Thank you, sir."

Emily retrieved her hand and wiped away tears as he bowed to the duke.

Hart turned back to the crowd. "It is no surprise to me that so many of you have come to care for Emily Spencer. I took her on as a pretend betrothed, a faux fiancé. And in the weeks since, she has made me laugh. She has demonstrated kindness and an incredibly clear insight that I can only envy. She has shown me true loyalty and awed me with her militant side."

He winked at the crowd. "I think we can all attest to her beauty—but I have had the extreme honor of growing to know her character."

The baroness let go of her other hand and stepped back. Hart took it up and bent over it. "With your great-uncle's permission, I would like to ask you, in earnest, if you will make the position a permanent one."

Emily laughed through her tears. She pulled her hand away and threw both arms around his neck. "Yes, my lord!" She tilted her head back to meet his gaze. "I would love to be your hired bride. Forever."

Epilogue

Hartsworth was indeed magnificent. It had two towers, a meandering river, an actual dungeon, glorious gardens and a great hall that made Emily dream of knights, troubadours and ladies in heavy, flowing gowns.

All of that was perfectly lovely, but in her estimation there was only one asset that mattered—and that was Hartsworth's master.

They had all gathered at the castle in preparation for the wedding. It was to be a huge affair. Everyone in Society wished to attend and sometimes Emily felt as if they had all indeed been invited.

But for now, it was just family. Emily and her mother had been put in the South Tower in a lovely set of rooms that had once been the Ladies Solar. The light was wonderful, the view amazing and right now—the occupants were worrisome.

Emily paced at the bottom of the Tower, around and around a pretty, wood-trimmed hall.

"That marble flooring has lasted hundreds of years," Hart told her. "But you are going to wear it out in an afternoon. Please, Emily, sit down."

"I cannot! I'm a bundle of nerves!"

"Are you going to be like this before our wedding?"

"No!" She crossed the hall, sat in his lap and kissed him. "The thought of marrying you makes me delirious with joy, not nervous."

"This isn't even your meeting," he said, settling his arms around her.

"I know. I was just so shocked when Mama refused to meet the duke."

"She did write him a very pretty Thank You for the help he gave us. He even let me read it."

"I know. It's just . . . I thought she'd been waiting for this her whole life. And once we knew that Danby meant us no harm, I thought she would jump at the chance to meet him."

"I think the reality of having a dream come true can be frightening," Hart said soothingly. "She only needed some time to think about it. And she relented and agreed to meet him before the wedding, so all we can do is be grateful."

"We can also be worried," she corrected.

A step sounded on the stair and Emily bounded out of Hart's lap to face the Tower. The duke emerged with her mother by his side. Emily watched anxiously, but her mother smiled and nodded—and Emily rushed to embrace them both.

* * *

She and Hart were married a week later in the great hall. On their wedding night Hart gifted her with her own personal library in the top of the South Tower.

"Glenna has agreed to help you fill it with all of your favorites," he told her between raptures. "I thought you would like it. You will need a new past time, after all." He grinned. "I've got the rents covered."

She laughed, remembering their discussion and threw herself into his arms. "I have a new vocation now," she whispered. "You."

She was very diligent about it too, and though it took a year and six months more, Hart's great-great-grandmother did come to visit Emily—and became a regular apparition for some time afterward. Their family was large and boisterous—and as should be said of an earl and his countess living in a castle—they lived Happily Ever After.

About the Author

USA Today Bestselling author Deb Marlowe adores History, England and Men in Boots. Clearly she was destined to write Regency Historical Romance.

A Golden Heart Award winner and Rita nominee, Deb grew up in Pennsylvania with her nose in a book. Luckily, she'd read enough romances to recognize the true modern hero she met at a college Halloween party--even though he wore a tuxedo t-shirt instead of breeches and boots. They married, settled in North Carolina and produced two handsome, intelligent and genuinely amusing boys. Though she spends much of her time with her nose in her laptop, for the sake of her family she does occasionally abandon her inner world for the domestic adventure of laundry, dinner and carpool. Despite her sacrifice, not one of the men in her family is yet willing to don breeches or tall boots. She's working on it.

Thank you so much for reading *The Earl's Hired Bride*. I hope you enjoyed it! If you are interested in hearing when my next book will be released, you can join my newsletter at **http://www.DebMarlowe.com**

You can also find Deb
on Facebook
on Twitter

And don't miss the other books in the Half Moon House Series

The Novels
The Love List
The Leading Lady

and Coming Soon:
The Lady's Legacy

The Novellas
A Slight Miscalculation
Liberty and the Pursuit of Happiness
A Waltz in the Park
Beyond a Reasonable Duke

And you can read Glenna's Story in the Danby book:
Lady, It's Cold Outside
in The Duke's Christmas Tidings